D

Proud! Domineering! Impatient! Demanding! Hot-tempered Nurse Saffron Pierce can list all Dr Jarvis Tregarron's faults on her fingertips, so when she falls recklessly in love with him, explosions are inevitable. But can prickly Nurse Pierce expect anything more than fireworks from the man she's christened *Dr Arrogant, MD*?

DR ARROGANT, MD

BY

LINDSAY HICKS

MILLS & BOON LIMITED
15–16 BROOK'S MEWS
LONDON W1A 1DR

*First published in Great Britain 1984
by Mills & Boon Limited*

© Lindsay Hicks 1984

*Australian copyright 1984
Philippine copyright 1984
This edition 1984*

ISBN 0 263 74863 4

Set in 10 on 11½ pt Linotron Times
03–1184–54,000

*Photoset by Rowland Phototypesetting Ltd
Bury St Edmunds, Suffolk
Made and printed in Great Britain by
Richard Clay (The Chaucer Press Ltd)
Bungay, Suffolk*

CHAPTER ONE

COMING out of the clinical room with a covered tray, Saffron almost collided with a tall, dark man who stepped briskly to one side to avoid her and walked on without a word or a smile. Bridling at the arrogance that had no time or interest for a mere nurse, she looked after him with a familiar stirring of dislike. Then, shrugging, she crossed the corridor to the room that he'd just left, ready with a smile for her patient.

She found Delia Tregarron in a flood of tears and Saffron's instinctive dislike and resentment of the man, a regular visitor, increased tenfold. The poor girl had enough to handle without him, she thought crossly.

As she reached the bed, Delia stretched out a hand to a box of tissues and tried to master the bout of convulsive weeping.

Saffron was moved to fresh sympathy. 'Whatever's wrong?' she asked gently, concerned. 'What is it?'

'Sorry, I'm just being silly. It's nothing—really!'

Heaven knew she had enough reason to cry, Saffron thought compassionately, smiling at her warmly. She had a soft spot for the girl who was so brave and uncomplaining despite the tragedy that had brought her into the private wing of the Howlett Memorial Hospital. But she only seemed to shed tears after a visit from one person in particular!

'Are you in pain? It's time for your injection, anyway.' She uncovered the tray to reveal the prepared hypodermic syringe and the gallipot of sterilising lotion.

'No . . . not more than usual.' Delia caught her breath on a shuddering sob. 'It's just—it's Jarvis!'

'I thought it might be,' Saffron said dryly. She took the slender wrist between trained fingers to check the fast-beating pulse. Curse the man! Delia was always upset by his visits and she wished she could tell him to stay away from her patient!

Everyone felt a great deal of sympathy for the girl, who'd been understandably confused about events and her identity when she was first admitted and didn't respond too readily when she was addressed as Mrs Tregarron. For only hours after she'd married Ivor Tregarron, he'd died in a car crash that had caused her own spinal injury. They'd been *en route* to the airport and a honeymoon in the Greek Islands when a faulty steering pinion had snapped and sent the car careering across the central reservation of the motorway. Assigned to nurse her, Saffron had struck up a kind of friendship with the girl, who was exactly her own age but seemed so much younger, so crushed by circumstances.

'He says I'm well enough to travel and he wants to take me back to Pethnavick. I don't want to go, Saffron! He doesn't understand, but I just can't bear the thought of going back to face his family without . . . without Ivor.' She said her dead husband's name on a gasp of anguish.

'It's much too soon!' Saffron agreed, swiftly in-dignant, hackles rising. 'Why, you're scarcely over surgery. Whatever is he thinking about?'

Delia had undergone delicate neurosurgery to remove crushed spinal discs and release trapped nerves that had temporarily paralysed both legs. Now, she faced weeks of physiotherapy to encourage her to walk again. Far from well, still suffering from the shock of the accident, she just wasn't ready to cope with the trauma and heartache of going back to Cornwall.

Saffron was incensed by the mere suggestion. Where was Jarvis Tregarron's sensitivity? His understanding? His compassion for his newly-widowed sister-in-law? He seemed to be thinking only of himself and the inconvenience of travelling regularly to see Delia and consult with her doctors. Selfish, unfeeling man!

'He says he's thinking about *me*,' Delia said heavily. 'I know he means well, but he doesn't understand, Saffron. He says I must go home eventually and it doesn't help to put it off. He says the family will be there to help me over the worst and I know they'll be kind. But they aren't *my* family and I'm sure they must blame me for what happened. How can I face them?'

'How could they possibly blame you?' Saffron soothed. 'You mustn't think that! I'm sure they all feel for you!' But privately she felt that if they were anything like the detestable Jarvis, they probably had just as little understanding or compassion.

'If Ivor hadn't married me . . .' Delia broke off, fresh tears welling. She covered her lovely face with both hands and wept.

Saffron coaxed her to stop crying and brought warm water to sponge her flushed face and soothe her hot eyes. Then she gave the injection that eased the pain and anxiety and settled Delia to sleep as it began to take effect. And all the while, Saffron was seething! Her patient was being treated for a very natural depression on top of everything else and she didn't need someone like Jarvis Tregarron to make matters worse!

Saffron suspected that the girl was nervous of such an autocratic and ruthless man who had a high-handed attitude to people and obstacles. She knew the type and he didn't frighten her! She'd enjoy telling him a few home truths if opportunity ever offered, in fact! But she'd been looking after herself for years and nursing taught a girl to acquire an extra skin and how to handle all kinds of people.

Delia had told her little about the man or the rest of the Tregarrons but she didn't seem to like the family she'd married into and she was obviously reluctant to make her home with them, as they apparently expected. It was certainly much too soon for her to leave the Howlett Memorial and throw herself on their doubtful mercies, Saffron thought, prickling with protective concern.

Leaving the room, she saw the tall figure of Jarvis Tregarron at the end of the corridor as he emerged from his usual conference with Sister and Dr Marks. He strode along the corridor towards her, obviously intending to spend a few more minutes with Delia before beginning the long journey back to Cornwall.

Instinctively, Saffron paused, waiting, her chin tilting and eyes unconsciously sparking with the desire to do battle. She watched him approach, unmoved by his striking good looks and disliking the scowling arrogance that marred his handsome features. Tall and dark, with piercing, deep-set eyes in a lean, intelligent face and a sensual mouth that resolutely refused to smile, he *was* good-looking—if one liked the type. The other nurses admired him, looked after him as he passed by, gossiped about his concern for the beautiful Delia, which brought him two or three times a week all the way from Cornwall to the outskirts of London.

Saffron wasn't impressed by the good looks or the physical magnetism of the man. She'd seen and heard enough about him to feel that his attractiveness was outweighed by the arrogance of his manner and his infuriating habit of looking through her as though she didn't exist. She suspected that he had scant liking or respect for women—and even less for nurses!

His glance swept over her, taking in every detail of the trim and provocative figure in the crisp blue cotton frock, the trifle of starched organza that seemed to be set so precariously on the burnished auburn smoothness of her hair and the militant sparkle in the clear grey eyes that met his own so fearlessly. He was in a hurry but he had time to feel a flicker of amusement as well as admiration for a nurse he'd noticed more than she probably believed.

'Mrs Tregarron is sleeping!' she said quickly, firmly, her tone implying 'no admission' as she blocked the doorway.

'I won't disturb her.' He put a hand to the door, disregarding the flash of annoyance in her eyes.

Saffron refused to move. 'I'd rather you didn't go in, Mr Tregarron.'

He raised a cool eyebrow. 'I dare say. But you aren't going to stop me.'

She put a hand on the handle of the door, quick and impulsive. His fingers closed over her own, steely with impatience. She jerked from his touch, flushing with anger and resenting the intimacy. He looked down at her, a glint of irritation in the dark eyes.

'You're behaving very foolishly,' he said coldly.

She took a deep breath. 'I'm protecting my patient. It's what I'm paid to do.'

'You surely don't suppose that I shall do her any harm!'

'I think you do a great deal of harm every time you come,' she told him bluntly.

'Just get out of my way!' he snapped, angry and imperious, losing patience. He thrust her aside and opened the door.

Saffron was furious. But she didn't have the physical strength to prevent him from entering. And she didn't really have the right, in view of the fact that he'd assumed full responsibility for the cost of the room and Delia's treatment, she reminded herself wryly.

She watched from the doorway as he went to the side of the bed and bent over the sleeping girl. Delia didn't stir. He looked down at her for a long moment and then he touched her cheek, briefly stroked her long blonde hair in a caress.

Saffron was startled by the look in his eyes and the seeming tenderness of his touch. She'd disregarded the gossip of her fellow nurses and decided that he didn't like Delia, hadn't approved of the marriage that had led indirectly to his brother's untimely death, and felt only a reluctant obligation to make her his responsibility until she was well again.

Now, she wondered if he *was* in love with his sister-in-law, as the grapevine rumoured, and if he had an ulterior motive for wanting to take her off to Cornwall at the earliest possible moment!

Jarvis turned to find her eyes on him, hard and suspicious. He moved away from the bed, impatient with himself for betraying an impulsive weakness for Saffron to witness.

He brushed past the hovering nurse and she closed the door very quietly. He looked down at her, glowering.

'Now, Nurse . . . What's all this about?' he demanded.

'You left Mrs Tregarron in tears,' she accused. 'Not for the first time, I might add!'

'She cries very easily at the best of times. It surely isn't surprising that my visits upset her? Hasn't she told you that my brother and I bore a strong resemblance to each other?'

Saffron stared, disgusted by the cool words that seemed to imply a callous indifference for the death of his brother as well as the feelings of his sister-in-law.

Incensed, she broke into words. 'You really are the most unfeeling . . .' She stopped short, biting her lip. It was against the hospital rules to quarrel with a patient or a relative and she had no desire to lose a very good job through this odious man. But it went against the grain to swallow her contempt, to bite back the longing to tell him just what she thought of him.

'She tells me that you want to whisk her off to Cornwall,' she went on, carefully controlling her hot temper. 'I don't think you realise that she's going to need nursing care and medical treatment for some considerable time.'

'Of course I realise it—and I have every intention of providing it,' he said impatiently.

Money no object, Saffron thought scornfully. As if *that* was everything! 'She'll need a lot of affection and understanding and compassion, too. Can you provide that?' she challenged angrily. 'You don't seem to know how she feels about losing her husband in such awful circumstances, or that she's afraid of facing your family. If you do know, you don't appear to care! It seems to me that you just want to order everything to your liking and convenience with very little thought for poor Delia!'

His dark eyes narrowed abruptly. 'I've given a great deal of thought to *Mrs Tregarron* and her needs,' he said coldly, emphasising the formality he expected from a nurse when she referred to her patient. 'You may believe that I know better than you what is best for her!'

'Do you think you know better than the doctors, too? Or nurses who've cared for her since she came here? What do *you* know of her physical condition or her state of mind? How can you provide her with the care and treatment that she needs if you take her away from one of the best hospitals in England!' Saffron was passionate with concern for her patient and dislike of the man's arrogant attitude.

Jarvis looked at her thoughtfully. 'What makes you feel that you have the right to speak to me in that fashion, Nurse?'

She stiffened at the silky menace in his drawling tone, the whip of scorn in the last word.

'Oh, I daresay you'll report me to Sister! But I had to say *something*! I think I care more about Delia—*Mrs Tregarron*—than you do. She's had a rotten deal and my heart bleeds for her. I wish I could do more for her—and I wish you'd reconsider and give her just a little more time before taking her back to Cornwall. She really isn't ready to cope with it, Mr Tregarron,' she finished urgently.

'*Dr* Tregarron.'

She stared. 'What?'

'I'm a doctor of medicine,' he told her coldly. 'Mrs Tregarron didn't inform you of that, apparently, and you weren't intelligent enough to check my qualifications before you questioned my decisions. It seems that you haven't heard of the Tregarron Clinic, either. It's an excellent private hospital, one of the best in the country. So you may be quite sure that your patient will have the best possible nursing care and treatment. I shall supervise it myself.'

Saffron felt thoroughly crushed. Knowing that she'd allowed her tongue to run away with her, disconcerted by the discovery that he was much better qualified than she'd known, she realised that he enjoyed her obvious discomfiture as he waited for the apology that she felt compelled to offer.

'I'm sorry,' she said, grudgingly. 'It seems I owe you an apology. I had no idea . . .'

The stiff words trailed off as he turned on his heel with the curtest of nods and not even the flicker of a forgiving smile. She didn't think he had a forgiving nature and she was sure that she'd made an enemy.

She watched with a sinking heart as he strode purposefully along the corridor to the door of Sister's office. He entered after a perfunctory knock and Saffron marvelled that she hadn't realised, from his coolly confident manner and his easy rapport with Sister and the eminent neurosurgeon who'd operated on Delia, that Jarvis Tregarron was a member of the profession.

She'd been so busy disliking him in the last few weeks that she hadn't bothered to notice the obvious pointers to the truth. It seemed that he had a certain standing in the medical world, too. She made a mental note to look up some information on the Tregarron Clinic at the first available moment.

It hadn't done her a scrap of good to challenge him, she thought wryly, and she'd failed miserably in her intention of helping Delia. She would certainly be sacked and she'd never see Delia on the road to recovery. And she'd never see *Dr* Jarvis Tregarron again, either, she told herself on a surge of relief.

She was astonished to learn later in the day that, far from complaining about her attitude and her abuse, he'd told Sister that he was leaving his sister-in-law at the Howlett Memorial for the time being as she was making such good progress and obviously getting all the tender loving care and attention that she needed from a conscientious nursing staff.

Sister repeated the complimentary words with an obvious glow of satisfaction. Saffron was sure that they'd been spoken in sardonic vein entirely for her benefit by a man who knew they'd be repeated in her hearing. Dislike of Jarvis Tregarron stirred even more strongly.

She avoided him as much as possible on his next few visits and he certainly showed no desire to notice her. But she managed to find out rather more about him from Delia—and she was stunned and shaken to learn that the lovely girl had been engaged to him before she'd married his brother.

Delia was naturally reluctant to talk about the circumstances that had led her to jilt one brother to marry the other. But, scarcely knowing Jarvis Tregarron and disliking what she did know of him, Saffron didn't find it surprising or strange that she had changed her mind about marrying him.

He struck her forcibly as an arrogant, harsh, self-centred and self-sufficient man, without humour or warmth, who didn't set out to be liked. Delia said that he lived for his work and that was only one of the reasons why she'd chosen to marry Ivor rather than him . . . and Saffron couldn't find a scrap of sympathy in her usually warm heart for a man who'd lost both bride and brother within a very short time.

It was inevitable that Delia should eventually be persuaded to exchange one hospital bed for another, of course. She wasn't the type to hold out against Jarvis Tregarron's obvious desire and determination to have her beneath his own roof, Saffron thought with understanding. And Delia was finally persuaded by his assurance that she would benefit from the ministrations of the Swedish physiotherapist he'd engaged because she employed new and effective methods in cases such as her own.

Delia made one stipulation. That Saffron should be asked to accompany her to Cornwall and offered a job at the clinic so that she might continue to look after her. During the weeks that she'd spent at the Howlett Memorial, she'd become attached to her nurse and increasingly dependent on her sympathetic friendship as well as her nursing ability.

Saffron wasn't surprised, having guessed what was in her patient's mind. She was a trained nurse with ortho-paedic experience and her other qualifications made her a very useful asset to any medical establishment. If it wasn't so, she doubted that Jarvis Tregarron would have agreed to employ her, for all Delia's insistence. For one thing, he had no reason to like her. For another, he was the kind to demand his pound of flesh from anyone who worked for him, she shrewdly suspected.

She needed very little persuasion to take the job. She had no close family ties and nothing to keep her in London and she felt that she was due for a change. She was fond of Delia and genuinely felt that she'd like to help her back to health. She'd made enquiries about the Tregarron Clinic and it had an impressive record. A nurse could never have too much experience in all kinds of nursing and it might be pleasant to spend the summer on the Cornish coast rather than working in a stuffy suburb, she decided.

The only drawback to the venture was Jarvis Tregarron . . .

It was a long journey by ambulance for both patient and nurse and Saffron kept a watchful eye on the exhausted Delia as the analgesic injection wore off towards the end.

'Not far now,' she said reassuringly, knowing that every curve and bump in the road meant pain and a feeling of nausea for the girl. 'You'll soon be tucked up in bed and able to relax. You've been very good but I'm afraid it's been an ordeal, as I expected.'

Delia mustered a smile. 'It hasn't been so very bad. Jarvis was right to insist that I came home, I think. I couldn't really put it off any longer.' She hesitated and added quietly, 'I know you don't like him, Saffron. But he only wants what's best for me, you know. He still cares.'

'Yes, I'm sure he does.' Saffron knew that Delia needed to cling to the comfort she obviously found in the thought. She marvelled that anyone could find anything to like and admire in the man. *She* certainly couldn't. 'But I still think it's a little too soon. He will have his own way, won't he?' she added, carefully light.

'You think he bullies me! I daresay I need to be bullied into making an effort. Nothing seems to matter very much any more—and no one understands that better than Jarvis.'

Saffron was rapidly tiring of hearing the man described in glowing terms. Affection seemed to blind Delia to the insufferable arrogance and undeniable tyranny of his attitude, she thought dryly. Just now, she was leaning heavily on him, turning to him, encouraging him to run her shattered life for her. Saffron suspected that he would take full advantage of every opportunity to do so.

'It isn't always possible to speed recovery in cases of spinal injury,' she warned. 'Nature must be allowed to take its course and damaged nerves need time to heal. I think Jarvis may be raising false hopes.'

Delia was making slow and careful progress but it might be weeks before she could manage more than a few painful, assisted steps between bed and wheelchair—even if the Swedish physiotherapist was the miracle worker that Jarvis declared her to be! Saffron didn't doubt the woman's qualifications or skill, but she did doubt Delia's whole-hearted desire to be really well once more.

'No, he isn't. I don't much care if I never walk again,' Delia said with a familiar bleakness that confirmed Saffron's thoughts. 'I do care about pleasing Jarvis. He's been so good to me. He wants me well and leading a full and active life again. Maybe he still wants to marry me—I don't know and he never even hints at it. But if he does . . . well, I can't help feeling that I owe him that much, Saffron. Nothing will bring Ivor back and I can't spend my whole life without someone to love me and look after me. I just can't!'

Even as her voice rose on the agonised words that Saffron felt had probably been lurking in her patient's mind for days, the ambulance turned through tall, wrought-iron gates and continued along a gravel drive lined by tall trees.

Saffron leaned forward eagerly for her first sight of the house, built of Cornish stone with mullioned windows and gabled roof and porticoed main entrance, surrounded by landscaped lawns and flower beds and set high on a cliff overlooking the sea. Lovely and gracious and very impressive, its beauty caught at her heart. At the same time, she felt an odd little surge of trepidation . . .

As she stepped down from the ambulance with a word for the driver, a plump, greying woman in a white coat, stethoscope dangling from a pocket, came out to greet them.

'I'm Dr Bellamy and you must be Nurse Pierce, of course,' she declared with no-nonsense briskness. 'How do you do? Welcome to Pethnavick.' She shook hands appraisingly. 'How has Mrs Tregarron coped with the journey? I'm afraid that Dr Jarvis isn't here at the moment. He's been called out to a patient.'

Saffron tried not to show her immediate resentment that the man had coolly gone out to a case that probably any one of his colleagues could have attended in his stead. It showed that he was just as uncaring as she'd suspected, she thought crossly, knowing that Delia would feel his absence at such a traumatic time. For herself, she couldn't care less. She was glad to postpone' the business of meeting him for the first time on his home ground!

CHAPTER TWO

AFTER a brief conference with Dr Bellamy about Delia and finding that she had a warm kindliness and concern behind the brusque manner, Saffron helped with the transfer of her patient from ambulance to wheelchair and along to the pleasant room that had been prepared for her on the ground floor of the house. Looking after Delia wouldn't be the full extent of her work, of course. She would be looking after other patients and working with other nurses, and so she looked about her and sensed friendliness as well as interest in the way that the nurses in their distinctive lilac uniforms nodded and smiled at her in passing.

Everything was very new but there would be plenty of time to familiarise herself with the place and the people. Her first concern was for Delia and she settled the weary girl into bed as quickly as she could.

'It's a gorgeous place,' she said warmly, having caught glimpses of foam-crested sea and gentle coves and golden beaches as the ambulance drove along the rambling coast road towards Pethnavick. 'The house is really lovely!'

'Well, I hope you will like it here. I don't want you to rush away, Saffron. I can talk to you—and I need you to see me through the first weeks at least.'

'Certainly I shall like it—and I've no intention of rushing away,' Saffron said firmly, busily unpacking Delia's toilet articles and the dainty cobwebs of lingerie and nightgowns that were more suited to a honeymoon than a hospital and had been intended for just that, of course. 'It's going to be a long, hot summer and I mean to enjoy every moment of it. Working in such lovely surroundings must be the next best thing to a holiday!'

It would be her first experience of nursing in a privately-owned clinic, but she didn't think it could be so very different to nursing in a state-run hospital. Surgical techniques and nursing procedures were fairly universal, after all. She certainly wouldn't be rushed off her feet and working the long hours that too many patients and not enough staff usually forced on hard-pressed nurses. There should be plenty of time and opportunity for exploring the coast and countryside and enjoying herself with new friends.

The open windows of the sun-brightened room admitted the sound of a car's tyres scrunching on the gravel drive. It was a very pleasant room with its french windows leading to a paved terrace and a rose garden but, seeing Delia stiffen, Saffron wondered if it was rather too near the clinic car park. She hoped that her patient wouldn't react badly to every car she heard, although it wouldn't be astonishing in the circumstances, she thought wryly.

Delia turned her head towards the window. 'I wonder if that's Jarvis?'

'Possibly. He'll want to see you looking your best,' Saffron said lightly. 'Just let me tidy your hair.' She took a brush to the soft fall of ash blonde hair that framed the lovely face and wished she could dispel the haunting sadness of the violet eyes.

The sound of Jarvis Tregarron's deep voice in the corridor, speaking to one of the nurses, preceded his appearance. He paused at the open door, an impressive man with his height and powerful build and sensual good looks. Saffron glanced at him briefly, still incensed by his absence on their arrival. He nodded to her, coolly formal, his dark eyes sweeping over her without apparent interest.

As he walked into the room, it seemed to Saffron that Delia shrank back against her pillows. Her frailty was emphasised by the man's strength and virility and magnificent masculinity, the seeming threat of his physical magnetism. Not for the first time, she wondered if Delia was slightly afraid of him. Seeing the frown that leaped into his eyes, she knew that he wondered, too.

Fair and very slight, with delicacy of bone and feature, pale beauty of hair and skin enhanced by the enormous violet eyes that were shadowed by suffering, Delia had an air of porcelain fragility that usually evoked chivalrous concern in the male breast. Observing the narrowed dark eyes and the slight tension of the sensual mouth, Saffron decided that it irritated Jarvis Tregarron and possibly evoked a streak of cruelty in his make-up.

He was an impatient and intolerant man who had little understanding of Delia's sensitive and genuinely helpless nature, she felt. Still in love with the girl who'd jilted him, he was probably unscrupulous enough to try and bully her into marrying him while she was too low in health and spirits to resist his autocratic manner and imperious will.

'Well, Delia, how are you?' He reached for her fragile-boned wrist and held it lightly, checking the rate of her pulse, eyes intent on the small, pale face with its trembling smile. 'I'm sorry I wasn't here to welcome you but Lady Elizabeth had one of her attacks and I felt that I ought to call. She doesn't pay a scrap of attention to anyone else, as you know. Did you find the journey terribly tiring?'

'No, I'm fine,' she assured him, the strain in the violet eyes and the pallor of the lovely face giving the lie to the words. 'Glad to be home . . .' The words faltered, trailed off.

He nodded. 'Glad to have you home—and we shall have you fit and well in no time, I promise.' He lifted her hand to his lips and pressed a kiss into the palm like a lover, with just the hint of a glowing smile in the depths of his eyes.

Saffron was astonished by such a totally unexpected gesture from a man who didn't convince her that he had a heart. It was unorthodox behaviour, too. Delia might be his sister-in-law. She might be the woman he loved. But he was attending her in the role of a doctor—and a doctor didn't kiss his patients under the very nose of an attendant nurse, she thought disapprovingly, wondering if she had suddenly become invisible!

'It wasn't a very pleasant or comfortable journey for Mrs Tregarron,' she interposed, more to remind him of her presence than to tell him what must be obvious to any doctor. 'She has a lot of discomfort although she won't tell you so, and I think she should have some pethidine and be allowed to rest.'

He swung to look at her, unsmiling. Saffron felt the waves of dislike and disapproval that emanated from him and wondered if he resented her influence over Delia. He must know that she didn't like or trust him and wouldn't hesitate to put a spoke in his wheel to protect the patient who was also a friend. She would probably be a thorn in his side in the coming weeks. He would have preferred to mould a broken-hearted and unresisting Delia to his will and desire without hindrance from a nurse who spoke her mind too freely and seemed to have little respect for his authority as doctor or employer.

'Why wasn't it given if it was needed? As I wasn't here to authorise an injection I'm surprised that you didn't speak to Dr Bellamy!' It was unmistakable reproof in the chilliest of tones.

Saffron bridled at the words and manner, which were more suited to a very junior nurse rather than one with her qualifications and experience. 'Dr Bellamy felt we should wait for your return and Mrs Tregarron insisted that she wasn't too uncomfortable,' she returned, chin tilting proudly at the implication that she didn't know how to care for her patient.

'I see.' Jarvis frowned. Saffron hovered like a dutiful nurse, hands clasped behind her back and just the right expression of demure deference pinned to her pretty face. But he didn't doubt the rebellion and resentment that seethed in her breast. 'Well, there's no need for you to chaperon, Nurse,' he said dryly. 'I want a private word with Mrs Tregarron. Run along and ask Sister for some pethidine—and you can come back with it in ten minutes.'

It was a dismissal that she couldn't ignore, but she strongly objected to his tone and mocking manner. Saffron went from the room, bristling with indignation but reminding herself with her usual good sense that if she alienated him entirely he would send her packing—and that wouldn't help or protect Delia at all. But she fumed as she went along the corridor, with its long windows overlooking the drive and the sweep of cliff down to the sea, and wondered if she could keep her tongue between her teeth where he was concerned.

He was the most detestable man! Quite insufferably arrogant! He hadn't spoken a single word of welcome or sent even the hint of a smile in her direction. He hadn't forgiven her for daring to challenge him on that first occasion and it was obvious that he didn't want her at Pethnavick. Well, he wouldn't drive her away before she was ready to go, Saffron determined grimly. She wanted to see Delia well and maybe even happy, and so she would stay for as long as it took—despite the fly in the ointment that was Jarvis Tregarron . . .

Sister Bronwen James was a soft-spoken Welsh girl with a warm smile and a readiness to be friendly. She had already introduced herself while Delia was being settled in her room. When Saffron found her in the clinical room and made her request for the pethidine for her patient, she seemed to welcome an opportunity to exchange a few details of training and nursing experiences, to tell the newcomer a little about the clinic and the way it was run and to talk about the tragedy that had struck the Tregarrons.

'Sad, it is,' she sighed, with the suspicion of a tear in her warm brown eyes. 'They were a lovely couple and so happy, drinking champagne and laughing about the confetti. She was so beautiful in her lace wedding gown and they were so much in love. It was a surprise to everyone when she married Ivor instead of his brother. But there—he was a lovely man. A friendly word and a smile for everyone, see.'

'Not like his brother, then,' Saffron couldn't resist, a trifle dryly. She was curious to know what others felt about Jarvis Tregarron. Particularly those who must know him very much better than herself, like Bronwen, who had worked at the clinic for some time.

Bronwen twinkled. 'Edge of his tongue already, is it? There's a good start for you! But you don't want to take too much notice of that old tongue, you know. Bark's worse than his bite. It just takes a little time for new faces to fit with our Dr Jarvis. Better than all over you from the first, indeed, like some!'

Saffron shrugged. 'Oh, it doesn't bother me. I'm used to the type that thinks nurses are dirt beneath their feet.

And the grab-and-grope brigade who think we're fair game!'

'Well, he isn't one of those,' Bronwen said firmly. 'I don't think he knows that we're women half the time. But he's a brilliant doctor and the patients trust him and he works very hard to maintain the clinic's splendid reputation . . .'

'Afternoon, Sister. And they say that listeners never hear any good of themselves! You *were* talking about me, I presume?'

They both turned. The speaker stood at the door of the clinical room, a man in his early thirties, fair and stocky and well-groomed in a formal grey suit, handsome and self-assured.

Saffron looked at him with a flicker of feminine interest. Inclined towards the romantic for all her level head and cautious heart, she knew that one day her destiny would walk into her life even if she didn't recognise it at first sight. So she was naturally interested in every new man she met—and this was a very good-looking one, with his smooth blond hair and blue eyes and ready smile, she decided.

'Good afternoon, Mr van Wyk.' There was the warmth of liking in Bronwen's demure and formal response. 'We've been expecting you. May I introduce our new member of staff, Nurse Pierce?'

He held out his hand, smiling with unmistakable interest at the slender girl with the rich auburn hair and creamy skin and clear grey eyes. 'It's always a pleasure to welcome a new nurse to Pethnavick—and particularly such a pretty one,' he said promptly.

Saffron found her hand clasped in strong fingers and a little warmth crept into her face at the flattering words and the blatant admiration in the bright blue eyes. An obvious flirt, she decided instantly, but attractive. And it was nice to be greeted in such a warm and friendly fashion after the cool hostility that was so unmistakable in Jarvis Tregarron's attitude.

'Mr van Wyk is our orthopaedic consultant,' Bronwen explained. 'We don't usually have the pleasure of seeing him so early in the week but he's come along today to see Mrs Tregarron.' She turned to the consultant, smiling. 'Nurse Pierce has travelled from London with Mrs Tregarron. She's been looking after her at the Howlett Memorial since the accident and knows all about the case.'

Saffron found that the man seemed rather reluctant to release her hand. Gently, she withdrew it.

'Dr Tregarron is with my patient at the moment. She's very tired and has some pain, but she stood the journey very well, better than expected. She's just about to have some pethidine.'

Suddenly realising that it must be more than ten minutes since she'd left Delia and her brother-in-law to their private conversation, she hastily reached for the tray with its prepared hypodermic syringe that Bronwen had laid ready for her while they talked.

The consultant accompanied her along the corridor to Delia's room. 'Do you know Cornwall at all, Nurse Pierce?'

'I had the occasional holiday here as a child and loved it. So I was glad of the opportunity to work in this part of the country—especially with summer coming. I'm sure I shall enjoy it and everyone seems to be very friendly.'

Not quite everyone, perhaps, she amended silently. But she didn't mean to lose any sleep over Jarvis Tregarron's unfriendly and unwelcoming attitude.

'We must do our best to make you feel at home.' Tom van Wyk smiled down at her admiringly. 'Perhaps you would like to come for a drive one day and I'll show you

some of our local beauty spots and entertain you to one
of our famous cream teas?'

Saffron smiled back at him. 'Why, yes, I'd like that,'
she agreed lightly, not too eager but warm enough to
encourage an obvious interest.

'Then we will make a date as soon as you've had time
to settle in.'

She was pleased with the promise. Of friendship as
much as an outing, she thought. This new man with the
Dutch name and the warm Cornish burr in his pleasant
voice was not only good-looking but he also seemed
rather nice. Knowing him might prove to be some
compensation for having to see far too much of the
detestable Dr Tregarron.

Saffron saw immediately that Delia had been crying
and she flashed an indignant glance at the tall man who
was standing by the french windows, looking across the
gardens, his hands thrust into the pockets of his white
coat and seemingly indifferent to the girl's distress.
Turning, Jarvis caught the militant sparkle in her grey
eyes and instantly counter-attacked.

'You seem to have a poor idea of time, Nurse Pierce. I
believe I said ten minutes.' Having delivered the rebuke,
he walked forward to shake hands with the consultant.
'Nice to see you, Mr van Wyk. It's good of you to come
along at such short notice.'

'Not at all.' The consultant strode to the side of the
bed. 'Delia, my dear . . .' He took her hand in both his
own and looked down at her with a great deal of
compassion in his blue eyes. 'You know how deeply I
feel for you. Ivor was my friend.' It was simply said but
the words held a wealth of sympathy and understanding
and shared grief.

Delia nodded. 'He had so many good friends. I was so
grateful for your letters and flowers, Tom. But everyone

has been very k-kind.' The slight stammer betrayed her
distress and the brave effort to keep back the tears.

'We're all very concerned about you,' he told her
warmly. 'You're very dear to our hearts, you know.' He
went on, more briskly, 'Now, I'm not going to subject
you to an examination today. I know you're very tired. I
shall come back tomorrow and we'll plan your campaign
of convalescence together. In the meantime, I'll have a
look at the X-rays and discuss your progress to date with
Jarvis—and your nurse, of course.' He included Saffron
with a swift and complimentary smile. 'I gather that she's
looked after you all these weeks and that will be very
helpful in assessing just how well you've progressed.'

'I don't know what I'd have done without Saffron,'
Delia said impulsively, emotionally. 'She's been a
wonderful friend and she's a marvellous nurse.'

'Well, now, I believe, she has something to help your
pain and then I want you to relax and try to sleep while I
take her away for a brief conference,' he said soothingly.

'Nurse Pierce is about to go off duty,' Jarvis said
firmly. 'It's been a long day for her and I'm sure she must
be anxious to relax and rest as well as unpack and settle
into her new quarters.'

Saffron stiffened. It seemed obvious that he didn't
want her sitting in on a conference between doctors. His
words relegated her firmly to a mere nurse who might be
foolishly flattered by a consultant's words and mustn't be
allowed to get too big for her boots. She certainly didn't
credit him with genuine concern for her!

'Then perhaps we should postpone our discussion
until tomorrow,' Tom van Wyk said promptly. 'I'm sure
that Nurse Pierce must have something of value to add to
it.'

'Just as you wish, of course,' Jarvis agreed indifferently.

'I'm so selfish!' Delia exclaimed, contrite. 'It just didn't occur to me that you ought to have gone off duty as soon as we got here, Saffron! You've been looking after me since early this morning and you must be tired out!'

'It's what I'm paid for,' Saffron reminded her lightly, wondering if she really looked as tired as she felt.

'Well, I won't have you worked into the ground,' Delia declared stoutly. 'Jarvis, you'll look after Saffron, won't you? I can rely on you to take care of her, I know. Everything must be so strange and new and she doesn't know anyone but you. Why don't you take her to dinner at that little French restaurant in Helston that I always liked so much? I want you two to be friends, don't forget!' It was light, laughing.

Saffron carefully schooled her expression as the doctor turned to look at her with a lift to his eyebrow as though he suspected her of prompting her patient into making such an outrageous suggestion.

She was just as surprised and indignant as he was, she thought crossly. Didn't Delia understand just how much she disliked and detested him and how much she resented being thrust on him that way? Fortunately, there wasn't the least likelihood that he'd obey that laughing injunction. The thought of spending the evening in her company must be as abhorrent to him as it was to her!

'If Nurse Pierce wishes to dine out after such a long and tiring day, then I shall be delighted to oblige her, of course,' he said, the sardonic tone implying the very opposite of delight.

'You're very kind.' Saffron's smile skated frostily over her lips and there was an unmistakable edge to her quiet voice. 'But I *am* tired and I do have to unpack and settle in, as you say, Doctor. I mean to have an early night.'

'Very sensible.' He turned to the consultant. 'The X-rays are in my office. I think we should go along and have a look at them and allow Delia to have a long overdue injection and some rest.'

As the door closed on them, Delia searched her nurse's incensed face with some anxiety. 'You look very cross. I suppose I said the wrong thing.'

'It wasn't very well done of you,' Saffron told her frankly. 'Forcing us down each other's throats won't make us like each other!'

'I suppose not.' Delia sighed. 'Perhaps it was clumsy. But I really do want you to be friends.'

'It isn't very likely, you know. For one thing, he's the big boss and I'm just another nurse. Can't you imagine what people would say if he took me out to dinner on my first night in Pethnavick? Or treated me differently to the rest of his staff? I'm perfectly happy with the way things are, believe me, Delia.'

'But you aren't just another nurse! You're a very special nurse—and you're my friend. That makes you a friend of the family, and why should it matter what people say? Jarvis knows how important you are and that I couldn't get well without you to look after me.'

If she really believed that, then it was obviously essential that she should stay until Delia was back on her feet in every sense of the word, Saffron decided as she gave her overwrought patient the injection of pethidine and left her to sleep.

She had nursed enough orthopaedic patients to know that psychological recovery played just as big a part as pathological recovery. An old lady living on her own, seeing no one for days at a time, might fall and break a hip and never get over it because she had no real incentive to walk again and no desire to return to a lonely way of life. Delia was young and her spinal injury was fortunately not of the kind to leave her unable to walk again—unless she chose.

It was vital that she shouldn't develop any kind of psychological block to the idea of being well and active, but the loss of her husband in such tragic circumstances could destroy a woman's desire to lead a normal life. Particularly someone like Delia, who seemed to need a man to run her life for her.

Saffron didn't doubt that there would be plenty of men eager and willing to take Ivor Tregarron's place in Delia's life. She was very beautiful and feminine and appealing. But it was possible that she wouldn't wish to remarry. At the same time, it was also possible that she could be coerced into marrying someone as familiar and as strong-willed and as dominant as Jarvis Tregarron.

Over my dead body, Saffron determined . . .

CHAPTER THREE

HANDING over the responsibility for Delia to one of the clinic nurses, Saffron thankfully went off duty at last, longing for a hot bath, a change of clothes and a meal. The sun still blazed out of a cloudless blue sky and it promised to be a lovely evening. She was hoping to explore the grounds or walk to the edge of the cliffs for a glimpse of the sea before she finally fell into bed to recover from the journey and the need to be constantly on the alert to attend to her patient.

Bronwen was just going off duty, too. 'Eight to four are my hours,' she explained lightly. 'I don't live in, see. I've a flat in Helston and a reliable little Mini.'

'Sounds a good idea,' Saffron said, feeling that *she* might be glad to put a few miles between herself and the Tregarrons at the end of the day.

'Oh, I don't know.' Bronwen took a last look round her office and closed the door. The two girls walked along the corridor to the imposing hallway of the main entrance with its sweeping staircase. 'I wanted to be near the shops and nearer to my boyfriend, see. But the housekeeping is a nuisance and Gary invites half the rugger team round at weekends and sometimes I think "there's daft you were, girl, to give up a lovely flat in the dower house and regular meals for the problems of this old place." So don't you do anything in a hurry now!'

Saffron smiled. 'I suppose most of the girls live in?'

'Well, it's convenient, isn't it? A few are local girls, living at home. But most of us come from foreign parts like yourself.' The warm brown eyes twinkled. 'Dorothy is a second mother to the girls at the dower house—in more ways than one! She's the warden. It's only a short walk but I'll give you a lift and introduce you, if you like.'

'I'd be grateful . . .'

'Nurse Pierce!'

They had just reached the open doors of the big house as the slightly peremptory summons rang out through the hall. They turned. Jarvis Tregarron stood at the head of the first flight of stairs, the light from the window behind him throwing his very handsome face into shadow. But Saffron didn't doubt that he was scowling, as usual.

'A word with you, please,' he went on in the arrogant tone that instinctively made her bridle. But she paused as he descended the stairs, quick and purposeful, white coat billowing behind him in the draught from the door.

'I'll wait for you in my car,' Bronwen declared tactfully. 'It's a brown Mini, too battered to miss!'

Saffron didn't take a single step to meet the approaching doctor. She wasn't inclined to meet him halfway in anything! His glance swept her from head to toe, impatiently. She felt that he didn't approve anything about her and her chin tilted slightly, defensively.

'What is it?' she challenged.

'My father wishes to meet you,' he said coolly. 'Oh, not at this very moment!' It was quick as he saw the protest form in her eyes, the shape of her mouth. 'The family dine at eight. My father would be delighted if you care to join us.'

He didn't make it sound like an invitation but an instruction. Saffron felt that he wasn't giving her the option of refusal.

'I'm rather tired, Dr Tregarron. I hoped for a quiet evening,' she reminded him.

'My father is over seventy and a semi-invalid and he retires to his room at an early hour. It won't be a riotous dinner party,' he told her dryly.

Nor very enjoyable with you glowering at me across the table, Saffron thought and almost said with her usual impatient candour. She swallowed the retort, reminding herself that she had to try to get on with this man. If only for Delia's sake.

'Very well,' she said with obvious reluctance.

Jarvis looked at her with a glimmer of understanding in his dark eyes. He knew he wasn't an easy man for a stranger to like or accept and it seemed inevitable that their very different temperaments should clash. But he couldn't allow her to challenge his authority—or undermine the careful control of his emotions.

'You don't yet know your way about, of course. Meet me here at seven-thirty . . .' Mary Bellamy emerged from a room on the other side of the hall with a folder in her hand and he walked abruptly away from Saffron. 'Dr Bellamy! I want a word with you about Mrs Farmer if you can spare a moment.'

Saffron turned towards the door, dismissed. He took it for granted that she would do exactly as she was told, she thought indignantly. Like a well-trained nurse! She wondered if he even knew that she was also a woman! He seemed to have no time for the normal courtesies or small pleasantries that greased the wheels wherever men and women worked together, and she didn't feel that there was an ounce of warmth or kindliness in him. Or humility! *Dr Arrogant, MD*, she thought scornfully, hurrying out into the bright sunshine to join Bronwen.

The engine of the brown Mini was purring gently as she slid into the passenger seat.

Bronwen glanced at her curiously. 'Problems?'

She shook her head. 'I've been summoned to the royal

presence,' she said lightly. 'It seems that Dr Tregarron Senior wants to meet me.'

'Dr Ben! Oh, he's a dear old man! He's very fond of Delia and I expect he wants to hear at first hand how she's getting on. He makes a point of meeting the new nurses, too. He's retired but still very involved with the clinic. Or was,' she added wryly. 'Losing Ivor hit him hard and he's suddenly become very frail.'

'I'm invited to dinner.'

'There's nice. Making you welcome, see!' Bronwen was intent on manoeuvring the little Mini from a tight corner and out of the parking area with its clearly defined bays.

'I suppose so . . .' Saffron was doubtful. She thought it much more likely that she was to be vetted by a formidable array of Tregarrons, who'd no doubt heard all about her friendship and her influence with Delia from an obviously disapproving Jarvis.

She'd learned something about the family from her patient. They'd been eminent members of the medical profession for many years in that part of Cornwall, it seemed. Twenty years before, Ben Tregarron and his brother Randall had founded the clinic, backed by a group of wealthy businessmen, and built it into a successful and highly respected centre for private medicine. Now, Dr Ben was retired and Dr Randall was dead and the clinic was run by the sons who'd followed in family tradition by becoming doctors in their turn.

Jarvis kept his very capable hands firmly on the reins, apparently. Ivor had been the resident anaesthetist. Randall's two sons, Clay and Philip, were surgeons, one specialising in gynaecology and the other in urology. Their sister was a paediatrician. Clay's wife was a nurse in charge of the theatre unit.

A family business in every sense of the word, Saffron

thought, dryly. Wherever one turned, one must bump into a Tregarron. And, if they were all like Jarvis, heaven help anyone whose face didn't fit! Herself, for instance . . .

She looked with interest at the small house that stood just within the gates, built in the same mellow stone as the manor house and set in a cluster of trees with its own trim garden.

'Staff quarters,' Bronwen announced, bringing the Mini to a careful halt. 'Known as Chastity Hall for reasons that will soon become obvious! Dorothy's eagle eyes ensures that all beneath its roof is as pure as the driven snow.'

'One of the reasons why you moved out?' Saffron teased.

'That would be telling, indeed!' Bronwen laughed. 'It's lovely, isn't it? It used to be the dower house in the days when Tregarrons were lords of the manor and still goes by the name. I suppose you knew that they go back to the year dot?'

It explained the arrogance to some extent. Anyone with his lineage, his family traditions and the wealth and influence and social standing that Tregarrons had prob-ably always enjoyed, couldn't help but be arrogant. No doubt it was bred in him. She might have been able to forgive it if only it was tempered with a little warmth and kindliness, Saffron felt.

She liked Dorothy Currie on sight. Tiny and bustling, she had bright eyes, rosy cheeks and a sweet face, a delightful accent and a warm personality. Saffron felt that she wouldn't mind at all being taken under such a good-natured and motherly wing, even if Bronwen did warn her that Dorothy's interest in her charges ex-tended to their love lives, too.

'I'm not expecting to enjoy much of a love life in the

next few months,' she returned confidently, smiling. 'The only men around this place seem to be Tregarrons and I'm not impressed by the one I've met so far!'

'Come to the rugger club dance on Saturday and I'll guarantee that you can take your pick from a dozen husky Cornishmen,' Bronwen promised.

'I might take you up on that!'

'I hope you do!' The little Mini moved off and Saffron watched until it passed through the gateway and turned towards the market town, ten miles away, feeling that she'd found a friend in the warm-hearted Welsh girl.

Her room on the first floor was small but very comfortable and welcoming with its chintz curtains and bedspread. The dower house had been cleverly modernised so that it lost none of its charm. There were an adequate number of bathrooms, a cheerful sitting-room for communal use and a well-equipped kitchen where the nurses could make hot drinks or snacks whenever they wished. Most of the day nurses were still on duty but Dorothy introduced her to two of the night nurses who were sunbathing in the garden.

Saffron was impressed by all that she'd seen so far and felt that the Tregarron Clinic compared favourably with any state-run hospital where she'd worked. The staff seemed to be efficient and well-trained, all the equipment was up to date and standards were apparently high. It had been the first of its kind in the county. Now, with the steady growth of private medicine, it was considered to be a reliable blueprint for others.

Her new uniforms hung in her wardrobe, frocks of the pretty lilac shade worn by the Tregarron nurses. She'd stuck out like a sore thumb in her traditional blue uniform, she realised. When she went on duty the next day, she'd blend into the background like the rest of the nursing staff.

In the meantime, she had to unpack and find something suitable to wear for dinner with the Tregarrons. She admitted to being slightly nervous. Jarvis Tregarron would undermine any girl's confidence, she thought.

She walked the short distance to the house to arrive punctually at seven-thirty, determined that he should have no cause for criticism. There was no sign of him as she entered the cool, high-ceilinged hall that extended to the back of the building.

Saffron waited, feeling self-conscious as a nurse passed in her lilac uniform and two men, obviously doctors, broke off a conversation to stare at her in open admiration. She'd put on a cool frock of cream cotton, its square neckline edged with cream lace and its short, puffed sleeves made entirely of lace to match. The nipped-in waist emphasised her slenderness and she wore a wide yellow belt that matched the bright yellow shoes and the yellow ribbon that she'd woven into the gleaming plaited coil on the nape of her neck. She wore the merest hint of eye-shadow and blusher and lipstick and, as a final touch, she'd dabbed some of her most expensive perfume on neck and wrists.

Young and resilient, she was much refreshed by a bath and a cat-nap and she felt she looked her best. She had no thought of pleasing Jarvis Tregarron, of course. So she was rather cross with herself for anticipating his arrival with a heart that beat slightly too fast.

The click of a closing door caused her to turn hopefully. Jarvis walked towards her, undeniably very attractive in the formal dinner jacket. He wore his dark hair slightly long and it gave him an unexpectedly rakish air, she observed for the first time. With his arrogant good looks and haughty manner and that cold reserve, he might have modelled for the part of Darcy in Jane Austen's *Pride and Prejudice*, Saffron thought.

She didn't smile.

His glance flickered over her briefly and then he frowned. 'I should have warned you that my father likes his guests to dress for dinner,' he said, without preliminary.

Saffron smiled then, very sweetly, chin tilting with a hint of defiance. 'I thought he might.' Her tone implied that she felt she was very suitably dressed for dinner on a hot summer night. She had no intention of showing dismay, but his words and manner almost destroyed the last of her confidence and her resentment burned.

A smile glimmered briefly in the dark eyes in response to the show of spirit.

'Never mind. I daresay it seems an old-fashioned notion to you, Miss Pierce,' he drawled. 'No doubt my father will think that you look charming.'

Saffron looked at him sharply, wondering if it was as near as he could bring himself to a compliment or if he was just being sardonic. The latter, she decided.

'Shall we go up? I meant to show you one or two features of the clinic but now there isn't time.' He swept on just as though *she*'d kept *him* waiting for nearly ten minutes. 'My father will be waiting.'

Dr Ben Tregarron sounded as autocratic as his son, Saffron thought crossly, as he ushered her into the lift that would take them to the private floor that was home to the Tregarrons. She moved pointedly from the light touch of his hand at her elbow, putting as much room between them as the small space would allow.

Jarvis looked down at her with both amusement and exasperation. He'd known that she was a pretty girl, of course. Now he saw that she could be beautiful as he admired the elegant coil of gleaming auburn hair, the creamy skin and the delicately lovely features of her heart-shaped face.

Her eyes, always so ready to flash fire at him, were her best feature, however. A clear and candid grey, wide-set and fringed with long lashes, always sparkling, very speaking. Intelligent and unafraid, like the girl herself. The family would like her, he decided. For himself . . . well, he had yet to make up his mind how he felt about Saffron Pierce. It wasn't easy to like someone so obviously determined to regard him with dislike and distrust.

She'd never forgiven him for putting her so firmly in her place. His nerve-endings had still been raw from the loss of Ivor and his anxiety about Delia, and he hadn't spared the nurse who'd dared to challenge him so unethically. He still felt that it had been unforgivable interference from a stranger, but he allowed that she'd been motivated by genuine concern for Delia.

She was silent, very stiff. Jarvis suddenly knew that he didn't have to like this girl to admit her impact on his sexuality. Desire stirred as he noted her tiny waist, the long line of her slender thigh and the tautness of her tilting, tempting small breasts beneath the thin cotton bodice of her frock. He was a man of powerful passions whose profession compelled him to keep his sensuality firmly under control. He ought not to want this nurse, so newly in his employ, with such a fierce and shafting desire.

But wasn't that really why he hadn't needed Delia's urgings to offer Saffron Pierce a job? Hadn't he wanted her from the moment when she'd confronted him, grey eyes blazing, hurling a challenge, trembling with an indignation that hinted at a passionate nature to match his own?

Not only wanted her, but determined to have her one day. By fair means or foul . . .

Happily unaware of the thoughts and emotions that

were concealed by the suddenly inscrutable expression of those dark eyes, Saffron looked back at him coolly.

'I understand that your father has been very ill.'

He nodded. 'Ivor's death was a great blow to him. They were very close. He is no longer young and the shock of hearing what happened caused him to have a slight stroke. He is very much better now, however.'

'It's been an anxious time for you,' Saffron said politely, but she privately felt that he had very little heart. He spoke so indifferently of his dead brother and his ailing father, and for all the love that he seemed to have for Delia he was often unmoved by her obvious distress. Hard and unfeeling, she thought, with dislike.

Stepping out of the small lift was like stepping into another world after the aseptic atmosphere and furnishings of the clinic, with its gleaming white paint, highly polished floors, array of medical equipment and bustling, efficient staff. This was the untouched part of the old manor house, giving a glimpse of a former and more gracious age. Family portraits lined the corridor and there were thick carpets underfoot, heavy brocade drapes at the long windows and beautiful tapestries hanging on the wood-panelled walls.

She stole a glance at Jarvis as they walked along the corridor. Dour and forbidding like so many of his ancestors, she decided, thinking of the dark portraits with their unmistakable resemblance to the tall doctor by her side. Had they really taken life so seriously and found it so hard to smile, those earlier Tregarrons? Was this modern-day scion of the family really as cold and hard and heartless as he seemed?

'I'm fond of Jarvis but he frightens me,' Delia had told her frankly. 'He's so ruthless. *If thy right eye offend thee, pluck it out* . . . That's Jarvis! He sets such high standards for everyone and if someone doesn't come up to them . . .' She'd sighed. 'He doesn't forgive, Saffron. He's so terribly hard . . .'

Intolerant, harsh and unsympathetic, without real heart. All true, Saffron decided. Physically very attractive, she admitted, reluctantly admiring his brand of good looks, the crisply curling dark hair and glinting dark eyes and the strongly sensual features of a lean and handsome face, the powerful build and the masculinity that tugged indefinably at her senses. But *personally* the least attractive man she'd ever met, she thought firmly, thankful that she wasn't a green girl who could be so stirred by looks and magnetism that she overlooked the flaws in a man's nature and personality.

Nevertheless, she wondered if Delia had some of it wrong. She had offended Jarvis when she jilted him so cruelly, but it seemed that he still loved her, still wanted to marry her. He'd forgiven Delia. For such a man to relax his own rigid rules must mean that he loved very deeply, Saffron felt. And that implied there was more to him than a stranger like herself could possibly know.

They entered a room that at first glance seemed to be overwhelmingly full of people. Saffron felt that all eyes were upon her as Jarvis led her across the room to meet his father.

Dr Ben Tregarron was very tall and still a handsome man with his silver hair and finely-etched features and warm smile. He had a great deal of charm that combined with old-fashioned gallantry to make Saffron feel very much a woman. She liked the twinkle in the old doctor's eyes as he shook hands and welcomed her to Pethnavick and scolded his son for not warning him that their new nurse was pretty enough to take an old man's breath away.

Jarvis smiled as though he didn't agree with the sentiment and went away to pour sherry for himself and

Saffron, while his father drew her down to sit beside him on the deep-cushioned sofa.

'Delia has told me so much about you in her letters,' Dr Ben said warmly. 'I'm delighted that you were willing to join us, Miss Pierce. I'm sure we shall all benefit from your presence just as much as Delia.'

'Well, I hope so, Dr Tregarron.' Saffron accepted the glass of sherry from Jarvis with a smile that was meant for his father and inadvertently included the son in its golden warmth. She didn't realise its impact on more than one man in that room.

'You must call me Dr Ben, my dear. Everyone does, you know. There are too many Dr Tregarrons in this part of the world! And here's another one of them anxious to push an old man aside to meet a pretty girl,' he added dryly as his nephew strolled across the room to join them.

Saffron was struck by the marked likeness between cousins. Clay Tregarron was just as good-looking in that very sensual way as Jarvis, and had his own share of the forceful physical magnetism that probably made them both attractive to women. But Clay was obviously a different type to Jarvis. He was warm and friendly and admiring. In fact, the glow in his dark eyes was rather too ardently admiring for comfort and Saffron decided that it wouldn't be wise to give him the slightest encouragement. She recognised the type too well. He was the kind who had a roving eye and probably roving hands to match, and she suspected that he was more interested in a newcomer than his elegant wife approved.

Meredith Tregarron was a slender brunette in a white satin dress that emphasised every curve of a splendid body. She'd been a theatre sister at the general hospital in Truro when she'd met and married Clay, and now she was responsible for the smooth running of the theatres at the Tregarron Clinic. With her striking good looks, self-assurance and obvious qualifications, she was undoubtedly an asset in many ways to her handsome husband. But Delia had hinted that it wasn't a happy marriage.

Clay's sister Fern, the paediatrician, didn't seem disposed to be friendly or welcoming, Saffron realised, as the tall, dark-haired girl took stock of her with a sweeping and comprehensive glance, allowed her a brief nod and a cool smile in response to the introduction and then turned away to talk to the staff surgeon who was another guest for dinner. Saffron smarted at the manner, which reminded her too forcibly of Jarvis Tregarron's arrogant incivility, and felt uncomfortably aware that her cotton frock compared badly with the elegant apricot chiffon of Fern's dinner dress.

Mary Bellamy smiled and waved to Saffron without leaving her window seat. Wearing classic black with a multi-coloured silk brocade jacket, she was talking to a young man whose looks and height and colouring betrayed that he was yet another Tregarron—but he went from the room before Saffron could be introduced to him.

The party was just about to adjourn to the dining-room when the tall young man returned. Throwing the door wide, he carefully manoeuvred a wheelchair into the room, complete with bravely smiling occupant.

'Fanfare of trumpets!' he announced loudly, so brightly that it might have been bravado.

There was a tense moment of obvious dismay and discomfiture. No one had known that Delia meant to join them for dinner that evening, Saffron realised.

Least of all herself . . .

CHAPTER FOUR

'BLOODY young fool!' Jarvis exploded, not quite beneath his breath. 'She isn't ready for this!'

Standing close to him, Saffron heard the furious words and saw the anger that darkened the lean, handsome face. For once, they were in accord! She agreed that Delia was far from ready to cope with a family dinner party. But it had obviously been planned between her and the 'bloody young fool', for she was wearing a long dress of dull gold silk and she'd taken pains to look her best, pale hair shining and her lovely face carefully made-up. It certainly hadn't been the impulse of the moment, Saffron thought shrewdly.

Delia looked strained but determined and it had no doubt cost her something to make the effort to appear for dinner after a long and tiring journey. The Tregarrons were formidable *en masse*, and she was meeting them for the first time since the tragic loss of her husband.

Saffron felt it was an indication of the family's feelings about her patient that only Jarvis had made the journey to visit her regularly at the Howlett Memorial. She could acquit Dr Ben of neglect for he was old and he'd been ill. But what of Clay or his wife or his brother—and what of Fern Tregarron? They were all close relatives and had presumably been fond of Ivor. Were they all such busy people—or merely indifferent to Delia's unhappiness and suffering? Didn't they like or approve of her, in truth?

Dr Ben was first to react more favourably. 'My dear

girl!' He struggled to his feet and went shakily to Delia's side. Taking both her hands, he stooped to kiss her and Saffron saw that the old man was much moved. 'This is a delightful surprise. No one dared to hope that you would feel up to joining us.'

'If this is *your* doing . . .' Jarvis threw at Saffron, glowering.

'It isn't!' The denial was swift and angry. How dared he suppose her to have so little thought or feeling for her patient that she'd suggest or encourage her exposure to such an ordeal so soon?

'Philip and I planned it between us,' Delia said, so promptly that she might have heard that low and angry exchange between doctor and nurse, so brightly that it was dangerously brittle. 'I couldn't let you dine without me on my first night at home. I'm not ill, after all—not now. Not even tired after a lovely rest. Jarvis, don't scowl at me! What harm can it do to spend the evening with my family?'

'None, I suppose. If it was really your wish and you weren't talked into it,' he said brusquely, instinctively reaching for her wrist to feel the throb of her pulse.

'I'll arrange for another place to be laid,' Fern said abruptly. 'Nice to have you home, Delia. Clay, give the girl a sherry. We're at least two drinks up on her!'

She went out of the room as Clay obediently turned to the decanters on the sideboard. His wife crossed the room to kiss Delia in welcome. Saffron saw the hand that rested lightly on Delia's shoulder in a wordless gesture of comfort and promptly decided that she liked Meredith Tregarron more than the others, who didn't seem to know how to deal with the situation.

'This is a sad home-coming for you, I'm afraid,' Meredith said quietly, speaking openly of the tragedy that had affected them all and that no one else apparently cared to mention. 'You must be missing Ivor terribly just now.'

Delia's eyes widened abruptly. Watching, alert, Saffron saw the blood draining from the beautiful face and shock stiffening the injured spine. She took a concerned half-step towards her patient and then glanced involuntarily at Jarvis for guidance. Should she or shouldn't she intervene? He hadn't moved or spoken, but the watching dark eyes seemed very intent.

'You've taken the first step towards rebuilding your life and I think you're very sensible—and very brave,' Meredith went on briskly. 'Facts have to be faced but it certainly can't be easy for you. If there's anything I can do to help—at any time . . .

Delia burst into tears. Deep, racking sobs shook her slight frame. She buried her face in both hands and gave way completely to the grief and despair that she'd been keeping so carefully under control.

For a moment everyone seemed turned to stone, obviously afraid of doing or saying the wrong thing and making matters worse.

Meredith looked down at the weeping girl with an expression of compassion and concern and then she turned away. Suddenly sure that she had deliberately provoked that fit of weeping, Saffron ran to kneel beside her distressed patient.

'You stupid bitch!' Clay ground the words between his teeth, glowering at his wife.

'Fools rush in . . .' Jarvis spoke with grim, sardonic censure in his turn.

'Someone had to say his name.' Meredith flushed at her husband's angry abuse but she stood her ground, coolly self-possessed. 'You can't shield her for ever, or make it easier on yourselves by behaving as though Ivor might walk through that door at any moment.'

Convinced that Meredith's motives had been pure, Saffron put her arms about the sobbing Delia and did her best to soothe and comfort her while the storm raged unthinkingly over their heads. Meredith was accused of all manner of things in the next few minutes, but chiefly the conceit of taking it upon herself to mention Ivor as though she was the only one who knew how to handle someone who'd lost both husband and health in one fell swoop.

Dr Ben had abruptly become a very old man, moist-eyed and trembling, his own grief welling anew at the reminder of the beloved son whom he'd lost so tragically. Fern abandoned her part in the attack on her sister-in-law to look after him, taking him back to his seat and talking gently and reassuringly to him, rubbing both his hands with her own.

Philip Tregarron said nothing at all. He stood behind the wheelchair, studying Delia as she wept, a stricken look in his dark eyes.

He so obviously felt responsible for the incident that Saffron was slightly sorry for him. Impulsively, she appealed to him.

'All this argument and emotion is so bad for her! Please help me to get her back to her room.'

He seemed to pull himself together at her words. He nodded. Then, seizing the handles of the chair, he wheeled Delia out of the room with Saffron hard on his heels.

As they left, she heard Mary Bellamy say briskly, in her matter-of-fact manner, 'She was near to breaking point, anyway. She would never have got through dinner, poor girl.'

'She'll need a sedative,' Philip said in the lift, running a hand through the crisp dark curls that betrayed his Tregarron blood.

Little whimpering sobs still welled from the depths of
Delia's misery as she huddled in the wheelchair, but she
seemed utterly unaware of her companions or her surroundings. She'd retreated into a private world of grief
and despair.

Saffron wondered about Philip as she looked at the
tall young man who didn't seem to be quite so much of a
Tregarron as the rest of his family. There was rather
more sensitivity and much less sensuality about the
finely-drawn good looks and the mobile mouth and the
eyes that were expressive of his concern for his cousin-
by-marriage.

'Why did she do it?' she asked him, puzzled.

'It seemed a good idea,' Philip said wryly, taking the
blame on himself. 'Putting it off would only make it
worse for her, I felt, and she agreed. We all loved Ivor.
We all mourn him. Meredith's right, Miss Pierce. We
must be able to talk about him freely—among the
family, at least. Bottling up the hurt doesn't help.'

'But she wasn't ready . . .' Saffron broke off, sighed.
How could she expect him to understand, doctor or not,
fond though he seemed to be of Delia! *He* hadn't been
with her every day for six weeks, nursing her through the
pain and the nightmares, encouraging the slow acceptance that still found it so hard to come to terms with
bereavement. 'We've just about managed to stave off a
breakdown all these weeks—and now this,' she said
wearily, despairing for the girl who was more friend than
patient.

'Perhaps this is just what was needed,' he suggested
quietly, almost hopefully. 'The catalyst of tears . . .'

'Catalyst, maybe. Catalepsy we can do without!'
Saffron said tartly, observing the wide, unseeing eyes
and the rigidity of the girl's limbs. She knew there was
some slight uncertainty about Delia's mental state

since the accident and there'd always been a danger that she might fall into that trance-like state of retreat from a world that she didn't want to live in without Ivor.

Delia was unresisting, apparently unaware, as she was undressed and put back to bed by Saffron with the help of another nurse. Without protest, she took the sedative that Philip had prescribed and then he stayed with her until it took effect while Saffron went to report to Jarvis.

She found him waiting to waylay her in the hall. Fuming, he was pacing up and down like a caged animal. Dark eyes blazing, he turned on her as soon as she appeared.

'How the devil did that come about? How did you allow such a thing to happen?' he demanded savagely. 'I brought you here to look after her, for goodness' sake!'

He wasn't making the slightest allowance for the fact that she'd gone off duty after a long and arduous day of looking after her patient, or that she'd known nothing of Delia's intentions. Her defences reared on the instant. *She* wasn't afraid of his tongue or his temper!

'I had nothing to do with it!' she flared.

'Someone obviously provided her with clothes and helped her to dress,' he pointed out harshly, patently doubting the denial. 'I can't believe that any of our nurses would be so irresponsible. My God! What fools women can be! First you—and then Meredith. Between you, she'll be driven into total nervous collapse!'

Two angry spots of colour burned in Saffron's cheeks and she drew herself up to her full five foot three with icy dignity.

'Your cousin is the one you should be reproaching, Dr Tregarron,' she said, trembling with fury, grey eyes bright with scorn. '*He* thought it would be a good idea. *He* made it his business to provide her with the clothes so that she would be suitably dressed for dinner. *He* told a

nurse—one of your *responsible* nurses—to help her to
get ready so that she could surprise you all. He aided and
abetted her in every way he could!'

'I'll wring his bloody neck for him,' he said. But her
fierce passion was cooling his own. Concerned for Delia,
suspecting that the independent Saffron Pierce had her
own and conflicting views on the best way to handle her
patient's return to normal living, he'd flown at her
unfairly, he admitted. He was quick but he could be a
just man—and he had no desire to set her against him
completely. A wry smile hovered as he looked down at
the girl who was rigid with justified indignation. 'It
seems that I owe you an apology.'

It was so cool, so stiff that she was even more incensed. 'Don't bother,' she told him coldly. 'It really
doesn't matter to me what you think.' She turned away,
proud and angry.

'*Now* where are you going, Miss Pierce?' he challenged sharply.

She looked back at him, chin tilting, bridling at the
impatience of his tone. 'To my room, of course.'

'Without your dinner? Don't be foolish. We've been
holding the meal for you and Philip. Where is he, by the
way?'

'With Delia.' She stared at him, more curious than
indignant. 'Do you really expect me to sit down with you
and your family just as if nothing had happened, Dr
Tregarron?'

'Certainly I do. I'm afraid you are not yet used to the
family rows—or the Tregarron temper. All sound and
fury, soon over and soon forgotten,' he said carelessly.

Saffron was infuriated by the air of indifference. 'And
it doesn't matter how they affect other people? I found
that scene not only embarrassing but quite incredibly
selfish,' she declared bluntly. 'You were all too

concerned with your own feelings to give a thought to Delia!'

'You're right, of course.' The casual agreement startled her and she looked at him suspiciously, suspecting mockery. 'We are all incredibly selfish and used to our own way in most things and we trample roughshod over everyone's feelings. So I'm not going to allow you to slip away, I'm afraid. My father has decided to dine quietly in his room and Dr Bellamy is going to keep him company. He's rather shaken, as you no doubt realised. Clay and Meredith are ominously silent. Fern is disapproving, as usual. Philip will be morose, nursing a guilty conscience, and I shall glower at him throughout dinner. So I need your presence to make the rest of the evening tolerable, Miss Pierce.'

It might have been a compliment from any other man, but Saffron was far from flattered by the cool, dry words and the lack of any warmth in the dark eyes. She found that he had her arm in a very firm grip. The strong fingers seemed to send a wave of tingling awareness through her from head to toe, a shock of reluctant response to the sexuality of a very masculine and very attractive man.

She wrenched herself free from his hold, resenting his high-handed attitude and his unexpected impact on her leaping senses. 'I can think of better ways to spend an evening,' she said tartly.

'So can I,' he returned. 'Particularly when I'm in a mood to dislike my family. Ivor was the best of us all, God knows! The peace-maker. Without him . . .' He broke off abruptly and she saw the throb of tension in his lean jaw. 'As you saw, we're at each other's throats,' he finished stiffly.

For the first time, Saffron knew that the loss of his brother had gone much deeper than she'd realised or he chose to betray. For the first time, she softened slightly towards him, her heart unexpectedly moved by that glimpse of his grief.

Jarvis Tregarron was a proud man who wrapped indifference about himself as a cloak, she thought with new awareness and understanding. Maybe she'd been too quick to condemn him as hard and unfeeling and insensitive.

But she hesitated. The prospect of the evening in store for them all appalled her. Then Philip came through the door behind them and checked abruptly as he saw Saffron standing with his cousin.

'There you are!' he greeted her, warm with relief and friendliness. 'I thought you might have gone back to the dower house. But you will stay for dinner, won't you, despite all the upset?' He turned to his silent and forbidding cousin. 'Jarvis, I'm so sorry. The whole thing was entirely my fault but I really thought it was for the best,' he said contritely. 'Delia was all in favour, too. When I told her that Miss Pierce was dining with the family, she wanted so much to join us. She said that Miss Pierce would see her through the evening.'

'You're a fool!' Jarvis said bluntly, without mincing matters. 'You knew her condition, her state of mind. I've stressed again and again that she's been close to a breakdown since the accident. Delia isn't strong. She can't cope with a number of things that other women would take in their stride. She's one of the world's dependents, you knew that! You knew she was likely to crack at a wrong word! Most of all, you knew that one of us was more than likely to say the wrong word! Tregarrons aren't noted for their tact, are they?' It was contemptuous, scathing.

'Meredith isn't a Tregarron,' Philip objected promptly. *Predictably*, too, Saffron realised, observing the flicker of slightly amused exasperation that crossed his cousin's handsome face. 'Who'd have thought that she could be so tactless, so unfeeling?'

'Maybe she caught the habit from Clay! Come along, Miss Pierce. We all want our dinner,' Jarvis said sharply.

He spoke as curtly as if Saffron was entirely to blame for the delay. Obviously impatient with an exchange that wasn't leading anywhere and had little point to it, he indicated with a peremptory nod that she should get into the waiting lift. She did so rather than continue to show her reluctance and possibly make matters worse for Philip.

She couldn't help feeling sorry for the young surgeon. Jarvis hadn't spared him—and he must feel quite badly enough about his part in the business without having coals of fire heaped on his head in front of a stranger, Saffron thought.

As soon as the lift doors closed, Jarvis strode off along the corridor, leaving Saffron to follow with his cousin. Intolerant. Harsh. Unforgiving. Rude. Yes, that just about summed up the detestable Dr Tregarron, Saffron decidedly indignantly, bridling at the arrogance that seemed to emanate from the broad back and the strong shoulders and the proud set of that handsome dark head.

Philip looked down at her ruefully. He had a sweet and rather boyish smile that was endearing.

'I'm so sorry. I'm afraid I've ruined your evening, and everyone was looking forward so much to meeting you and thanking you for all you've done for Delia. Her letters have been full of you all these weeks, you know. She declares that you saved her life.'

Saffron shook her head, smiling. 'Oh, what nonsense! I just did my job. The doctors saved her life. That's *their* job, isn't it?' She looked up at him with a quick warming of her smile that admitted his superior qualifications as doctor and surgeon.

'Her sanity, then,' Philip persisted.

'She needed a friend as much as a nurse. I just happened to be there and we took to each other,' Saffron said simply. She added impulsively, 'Like to like, maybe. We were born under the same star. On the very same day, in fact. So we had something in common and built on that.'

'It's about all that you do have in common, I imagine,' Jarvis said bluntly, overhearing and checking his pace so that they caught up with him. 'You're entirely different types. You are capable and independent and self-sufficient—all the things that make a good nurse.' It was too careless to be a compliment. 'While Delia can scarcely look after herself, let alone anyone else! She feels things very deeply, too. She needs a lot of affection and understanding and caring concern. Just as you once informed me, Miss Pierce,' he added.

'And you think that nurses *don't!*' It was quick, indignant. Saffron had suffered before from the common belief that nurses were cast in a different mould to other women.

Jarvis said nothing. He threw open the door of the drawing-room and Saffron entered with some reluctance and slight trepidation.

Fern Tregarron tossed aside a magazine and rose promptly to her feet. 'At last! I'm famished.'

'How is Delia?' The anxious query came from Meredith as she left the piano, where she had been playing softly for her own comfort and pleasure.

'Under sedation,' Jarvis said curtly.

'Do *you* believe that I wanted to hurt her?' she challenged swiftly.

'For goodness' sake, Meredith, not now!' he said impatiently. 'This is all very tedious for Miss Pierce.'

'I doubt it,' Clay drawled before Saffron could speak

for herself. He turned from the window, glass in hand, and his dark eyes rested on the new nurse. 'Miss Pierce is as closely concerned as any of us, Jarvis. If you'd read Delia's letters you would know that she looks upon her as a very dear friend. In my book, that makes her a friend of the family.' He strolled across the room to Saffron and offered his arm to her, smiling. 'You must be longing for your dinner . . .'

'Yes! For heaven's sake, let's eat,' Fern echoed the suggestion thankfully, heading for the dining-room.

Saffron glanced at Meredith with a hint of doubt in her grey eyes. Then she slipped her hand through Clay Tregarron's arm. She didn't mean to encourage him but she was grateful for the friendly gesture that defended her against another man's deliberate policy of treating her like an outsider and an enemy.

Dinner wasn't the ordeal that she'd expected it to be. With Clay on one side and Philip on the other, both attentive and doing their best to make her feel at ease, she could overlook the fact that Jarvis Tregarron's smouldering gaze was frequently and critically upon her during the meal.

She wondered why he'd been so insistent on her presence, only to virtually ignore her! She felt that he didn't approve of Clay's flattering attentiveness to her or Philip's warm and friendly interest, but *he* made no effort to please or entertain her.

To be fair, he scarcely spoke to anyone, she conceded. He ate little and helped himself liberally to the wine and sat regarding them all with a glitter of scornful mockery in the deep-set dark eyes.

If he liked them all so little, why on earth did he remain so closely involved with the clinic and his family, Saffron wondered dryly. Why hadn't he left to live a life of his own long before?

He was a strange, enigmatic man. It wasn't so surprising that Delia had found it impossible to marry him, she decided.

The thought coincided with a clash of their eyes across the dinner-table. His penetrating gaze seemed quite capable of reading her mind, Saffron thought resentfully. But she looked back at him coolly, proudly. He might be able to browbeat Delia. His family might be wary of the harsh tongue that didn't seem to care how it hurt or offended. But *she* wasn't afraid of him. He had no power to hurt her in any way. The worst that he could do to her was to dismiss her from his staff—and she didn't think he would do that while Delia needed her.

For he was certainly very much in love with the beautiful and sensitive Delia . . .

CHAPTER FIVE

LATER that evening, over coffee and liqueurs in the drawing-room, Saffron sat with Meredith Tregarron in animated conversation. A chance remark had revealed that they were both Kit's nurses and they were deep in discussion of their training days, discovering a dozen or more mutual acquaintances and exchanging a spate of lively anecdotes about nursing.

Saffron had been slightly surprised when Meredith came across the room to join her with a friendly smile, for Clay had been neglecting his wife all evening. She thought it was probably a common state of affairs. She didn't much like Clay Tregarron. Fortunately, his very likeable wife didn't seem to suspect her of encouraging him and Saffron hoped that she'd found another friend.

Under cover of the conversation, Meredith said softly, 'I wasn't being cruel to Delia, you know.'

'I *do* know.' Saffron smiled warmly, reassuring. 'I acquitted you of that right away. Shock tactics work very well sometimes and tears can be therapeutic. But I'm afraid that Delia's hurt goes much deeper than any of you possibly realise. She wasn't just very much in love with Ivor . . .'

She hesitated briefly and then went on quietly, 'I don't mean to be presumptuous, but I think she also relied on him to support her against his family. Now she feels lost and afraid and terribly anxious about the future.'

'Poor little Delia,' Meredith said in rather a cryptic tone.

Saffron glanced at her quickly. 'Isn't she?'

The slight shrug of Meredith's slim shoulders was expressive. 'I'm desperately sorry for her, of course,' she said carefully. 'Isn't everyone? It was a terrible thing to happen. But she'll land on her feet, you know. That type always does—haven't you noticed? There's always someone to pick up the pieces and take care of damsels in such obvious distress. Oh, dear! Now you'll think that I'm just being spiteful,' she added ruefully as Saffron stiffened.

'Aren't you?' she challenged bluntly. She wondered if Meredith also saw Jarvis Tregarron in the role of white knight, riding to Delia's rescue—and if she could possibly be jealous.

'No. I'm as fond of Delia as everyone else—and she does inspire genuine affection,' Meredith returned, patently sincere. 'Maybe I'm still a little cross with her for doing the dirty on Jarvis.' The frank words betrayed affectionate concern for her husband's very attractive cousin, if nothing more. 'But I didn't blame her for marrying Ivor. He really was the nicest man—and heaven forbid that I should feel she deserved to lose him so tragically!'

'No one deserves that kind of suffering,' Saffron agreed, wishing she knew just how Delia had 'done the dirty' on Jarvis and knowing that she couldn't ask.

Philip interrupted their muted conversation at that point, approaching them eagerly. 'Do you play bridge, Saff—Miss Pierce?'

'Yes, I do. But not very well, and not tonight, if you don't mind.' She smiled at him. His obvious impatience with formality, betrayed by the slip of a tongue that seemed to be longing to use her first name, was endearing. 'I'm really rather tired and longing for my bed.' She got to her feet, adding lightly, 'Don't you think you could call me Saffron—off duty, at least? Even if we haven't been formally introduced.'

He laughed. 'Then you must call me Philip,' he said warmly. 'First names all round, then. Much more friendly. Don't you agree, Jarvis?'

He appealed to his cousin, who lounged in a deep armchair, nursing a drink, long legs outstretched and heavy-lidded eyes almost closed, taking no part in any of the conversation and making no attempt to appear other than utterly bored with the company.

'Oh, certainly,' he roused himself sufficiently to drawl, his tone indifferent. He set down his drink and looked round at Saffron. 'Leaving, Miss Pierce? I'll walk to the dower house with you.'

It wasn't the courteous, kindly offer of a thoughtful and considerate host. It was more in the nature of a command and the formal address followed so swiftly on Philip's warm suggestion that it seemed deliberately pointed to offend. His manner seemed to imply that his family could do as they pleased but he had no intention of including her among his friends. Saffron was glad that it didn't matter to her. She didn't need the liking or the approval or the admiration of a man like Jarvis Tregarron, with his scornful tongue and hard eyes and infuriating arrogance.

'Thank you. But it's only a step and I won't put you to the trouble,' she said crisply, very cool.

He was already on his feet. 'No trouble. I can use the exercise.'

'Let *me* escort you, Saffron!'

Both men spoke at the same moment, one almost offensively casual, the other too-eager by contrast. The lift of an arrogant eyebrow put the younger man promptly in his place.

'You've done quite enough escorting for one night,

Philip.' The heavy irony of the words brought a flush to the surgeon's cheek.

'We need you to make up a four, anyway,' Fern interposed briskly, settling the matter. 'Jarvis won't play.'

Jarvis turned to her and inclined his head in ironic agreement. 'Very perceptive of you, Fern,' he drawled mockingly. 'Jarvis *won't* play. Not tonight or any night. You may bicker freely among yourselves and hold as many post-mortems as you wish without me. I won't be back. I've some paperwork to do in the office.' He turned back to Saffron, unsmiling. 'You'll need a wrap, Miss Pierce. The breeze from the sea strikes chilly at night as it sweeps across the cliffs. Meredith, I'll borrow this if I may . . .' He reached for a soft silk stole that lay over a chair.

'Yes, of course—take it.' Scarcely glancing at him, she gave absent permission, already dealing the cards for the first hand of bridge.

Saffron wondered if Clay's attractive, sophisticated wife welcomed a relief from the boredom of a family evening. If this one was typical, with its many undercurrents to accompany the tedium that Jarvis certainly made no effort to dispel, then she wouldn't care to be married to a Tregarron, she decided firmly.

Going down in the lift with him she was silent, avoiding the disconcertingly direct gaze of dark eyes that seemed to be resting on her with a kind of challenge in their enigmatic depths. She was much too aware of him in that confined space. He was disturbingly attractive, and she didn't have to like him to admit to a slight kindling of entirely physical interest.

Jarvis was conscious of her nearness and her warm, enchanting femininity. The delicate perfume that emanated from her hair and slender body was teasing and exciting his senses. He'd been drinking rather more than usual and he felt reckless. He wanted to reach for her then and there, risking the inevitable rebuff. The lift doors opened just as desire stirred strongly with sharp and insistent wanting.

The night air stung with cool, slightly salt spray on Saffron's face and bare arms and the strong breeze ruffled the soft curls that clamoured about her temples. She welcomed the refreshing coolness after the stuffiness of the house and the tensions of the evening.

Jarvis came up behind her and she felt the touch of his hands as he draped the thin stole about her shoulders. Incredibly, she thought that his hands stilled and lingered for a moment. For absolutely no good reason, her heart quickened with a strange and very foolish anticipation that was almost excitement, and a little tremor shivered down her spine.

'You're cold,' Jarvis said, without apparent concern.

'Just a little.' Saffron began to walk on and he fell into step by her side, his shoes scrunching on the gravel. They strolled away from the shadows of the big house with its lighted windows and muted bustle of nurses going about their routines while patients slept.

It was a very dark night, the moon hiding behind a bank of black velvet cloud. The tall trees loomed above their heads as they walked towards the dower house, situated at the end of the long drive. It was so breathlessly still that Saffron could almost hear the unsteady thump of her heart.

She felt a tingling awareness of the man at her side, so tall that her head only just reached his shoulder, so masculine that he seemed to spark an unexpected and very alarming echo to his magnetism in the depths of her being. It was disturbing to realise the powerful tug of physical attraction for a man she scarcely knew and didn't like at all.

An owl suddenly hooted, near enough to make her start and move involuntarily closer to him. She sensed rather than saw the sudden flicker of a smile that warmed his handsome face.

'Town girl,' he mocked.

'Wrong!' she snapped, pleased to set him right. He was much too quick with his conclusions. 'I was born and bred in the country.'

'Were you, indeed? Which part of the country, Miss Pierce?'

'Norfolk—and couldn't you just call me Saffron, like everyone else?' she demanded with sudden impatience, annoyed that he continued to keep her so severely at a distance—and even more annoyed to realise how much she minded the formality of his attitude.

But the circumstances dictated a different kind of relationship to the usual one between doctor and nurse or between employer and employee, she felt. Whether Jarvis Tregarron liked it or not, she had been received as a friend by the rest of his family. They'd obviously be thrown together more often than either of them might wish in the coming months and they might as well make the best of it.

Besides, having clashed with a fury that brought a degree of intimacy to their mutual dislike, they couldn't now behave like strangers. They had to be either friends or sworn enemies. Saffron was prepared to bury the hatchet if he would. Not because she liked him but because she didn't like to be on bad terms with anyone.

'Saffron,' he mused, as though trying it for size on his tongue. 'Saffron . . .' Low, lingering, his deep voice almost turned her name into a murmur of endearment and she stiffened, shooting a glance at him that was half-startled, half-suspicious. He looked down at her coolly. 'Yes, I daresay I will use it at suitable moments,' he agreed with that infuriating arrogance.

Her hackles rose. 'When you feel disposed to be friendly? You aren't likely to wear it out, in that case!' she said.

Jarvis laughed suddenly, softly. Saffron realised that she'd risen to the bait just as he'd intended and she glowered. Difficult, detestable man! She stalked at his side in angry silence, longing for an end to this enforced tête-à-tête.

After a few moments, he spoke again. 'You're a long way from home. Do you have any family? Parents? Brothers or sisters?'

He wasn't the type to make idle conversation and Saffron was slightly surprised by the interest he was taking for the first time in her background.

'Father. One sister, three years older,' she said coolly. 'We aren't close and I don't see them very often. My mother died when I was eleven and I was sent to live with a grandmother in London. But Felicity had just begun to be useful about the farm and so she stayed with my father. She's married and I'm due to become an aunt for the first time in the autumn.'

'What about you? Do you have any plans in that direction? A fiancé in the background, for instance?'

'No. Not even a steady boyfriend at the moment. If there was someone, I wouldn't be here—even to please Delia.' She shot another glance at him. 'Why do you ask?'

He shrugged. 'Curiosity. Men obviously find you attractive.'

The drawling tone flicked her on the raw. It seemed to sneer at Clay's readiness to draw her into the family circle and pay her so much attention and at Philip's more acceptable interest and warm friendliness.

'It seems to surprise you!' she snapped, instantly on the defensive.

'Not at all. You're a good-looking girl,' he said carelessly.

'It's kind of you to say so,' she said sweetly, fuming Damned with faint praise, she thought, indignant.

'Kind?' Jarvis shook his head. 'I'm not a kind man. I'm too blunt for most people and I don't readily tolerate the weak or the foolish. You saw that for yourself this evening.'

'I saw and heard the way you treated your cousin, if that's what you mean.' Saffron instantly flew to the defence of Philip, whom she'd liked almost on sight. 'You were much too hard on him! I'm sure he meant well.'

'Heaven preserve me from the well-meaning,' he retorted dryly. 'I've suffered too much from them for years. If only good intentions could occasionally be combined with good sense, we should all sleep more soundly in our beds at night.' He added wryly, 'God knows what harm he's done Delia with his well-meaning interference!'

'The real harm was done when you brought her back to this place with all its memories and reminders of Ivor,' Saffron told him bluntly. 'It was heartless, I think—and dangerous considering her state of mind!'

If he didn't like plain speaking then he shouldn't have offered her a job at the clinic, she thought, sensing that he stiffened. He knew that she didn't hesitate to say what was on her mind any more than he did!

'Delia wanted to come home. It was her wish,' he said impatiently.

'Just as she wanted to join the family for dinner?' It

was quietly sardonic. 'You know perfectly well that she really wanted to please Philip! Just as she agrees to everything that you want in order to please you! For different reasons, however. She seems to be very fond of your cousin. She's so anxious not to offend you in any way that I'm inclined to believe that she's frightened of you!'

'For an intelligent girl and a trained nurse, you talk a deal of nonsense,' he said curtly. 'Delia's desire to please is a very endearing trait—and it's one that *you* would be well advised to acquire if we are ever to get along, Miss Pierce.'

Saffron looked at him with acute dislike. 'Pleasing you isn't written into my contract, fortunately—and *I'm* not frightened of you. You won't walk over me as you do Delia! You don't make or mar the day for me with a word or a look as you do for Delia! I don't think you have the slightest idea how to handle her or how she feels about you.'

'That's enough. Don't say any more—not unless you wish to make me really angry,' he said sharply, roused at last. 'How dare you set yourself up as an authority on Delia's feelings after a few short weeks? I know her very much better than you do and I know exactly how she feels about me!'

Startled by that sudden flame of anger, Saffron came to an abrupt halt. 'We'd better say goodnight before we come to blows, Dr Tregarron,' she said stiffly. She whisked the stole from her shoulders and held it out to him with a dismissive air. 'Please give this back to Meredith, with my thanks.'

The moon chose that moment to make a belated appearance, drawing aside the dark clouds to sail across the sky in silvery splendour. Its pale glow illumined the couple who confronted each other beneath the trees, falling across the man's handsome head and lighting the proud and pretty face that was tilted to meet the challenge of his anger.

She was more than pretty in the moonlight that trembled on her face and hair and the swell of her breasts that rose and fell with her quickened breathing. Jarvis looked down at her and his expression changed abruptly as desire surged anew. He reached for her wordlessly.

Saffron just had time to recognise the intent that replaced the anger in his eyes before he caught her hand and drew her against him and kissed her, quick and hard, forcing the breath from her body with the shock of that unexpected contact with his powerful frame. Meredith's stole lay forgotten where it fell as their lips clung and quickened for a breathless moment of time.

Then Jarvis released her, just as abruptly as he'd caught her close. Saffron stared at him, more in surprise than affront. He was quite ruthless, she realised. What he wanted he apparently took without a thought for anything but the satisfaction of his desires, his aims, his ambitions. A dangerous man. But what really alarmed and shocked her was the knowledge that his passion had evoked a leaping flame of desire such as she'd never known, and that she was filled with longing for the ecstasy and the fulfilment that his kiss had seemed to promise.

'Goodnight, Saffron . . .' He turned and strode back along the drive towards the house without another word.

Saffron looked after him, puzzled and dismayed. Why hadn't she slapped that arrogantly handsome face? Why had she allowed him to kiss her without a word of protest? Why had she let him walk away as though she didn't mind being kissed by a virtual stranger?

Most important of all, why had she melted at his

touch, his kiss, the glow in his eyes, and kissed him back in swift and eager response?

Troubled, she walked on to the dower house and made her way up to her room, thankful not to meet Dorothy or any of her fellow nurses.

It had been a horrid evening from start to finish, she thought crossly, slipping her frock on to a hanger and storing it in the wardrobe, then sitting down at the dressing-table to unbraid her hair. Jarvis Tregarron had taken it for granted that she wouldn't object to being kissed by him. Did he think she liked him, was interested in him, would welcome his amorous advances? Heaven forbid! He wasn't her type at all!

He was infuriatingly high-handed, believing that he could say and do exactly as he pleased without a thought for anyone's feelings. Despicable, detestable juggernaut of a man. *Dr Arrogant MD*!

Curled in a tight ball between the sheets, she was too tired from the tensions and demands of a very long day to slip easily into sleep. A shaft of moonlight fell across her bed through the window and threw the shadows of the furniture into relief against a wall. One of the shadows bore a marked resemblance to Jarvis Tregarron's distinctively handsome head, Saffron discovered, her heart giving an odd little bump of alarm. She sat up quickly and found it was the shadow of a small bronze bust of Byron that stood on a table by the window.

She thumped her pillows and settled down once more to chase the elusive sleep that she needed so much if she was to do her work properly the following day. She tried to channel her thoughts in the right direction but no matter which way they went they continually led back to Jarvis Tregarron. In the end, she gave up the unequal struggle and allowed herself to dwell with remembered delight on the way he'd held and kissed her, meaningless though it had been for a man who was in love with another woman, foolish though it was to be so stirred by the physical attractions of a man she didn't even like.

And it was even more foolish to wake in the morning to realise that the night had been filled with restless and disturbing dreams that she certainly wouldn't want to come true!

Smoothing the crisp linen over her hips, Saffron admired the tailored lines of the lilac frock that gave the Tregarron nurses a distinctive touch of class. She secured the neat little cap with strategically placed hairpins and brushed back a strand of her gleaming auburn hair. She was almost ready for her first official day on duty at the Tregarron Clinic. But far from ready to meet Jarvis Tregarron again, she admitted.

Delia was awake but apathetic when she went into her room a little later. She didn't even have a smile for Saffron, who had been surprised to learn from one of the night nurses that Jarvis had spent the greater part of the night beside her patient's bed.

Saffron wondered if he'd been troubled by a degree of guilt because he'd succumbed to the temptation to make love to another woman. It was much more likely that he didn't mean to miss any opportunity to convince Delia that she needed his love and support, she told herself dryly. A man like Jarvis Tregarron wouldn't attach any importance to a fleeting fancy for someone else. He would simply take what he wanted and never give it another thought. The best thing that she could do was to forget it, too.

She tried to rouse Delia with warm, friendly chat as she coaxed her out of bed and into a dressing-gown and wheeled her through the french doors into the welcoming sunshine of another beautiful day. The flower beds were a mass of bright and lovely colour. The well-kept lawns were very green. Birds were trilling happily in the trees and the sparkle of the sun on the distant sea ought to have brought a lift to the lowest spirits.

Delia was unmoved by it all. Every lovely day was another reminder of the way the sun had shone on her wedding day. It was another day that she couldn't share with Ivor. But at least she wasn't as withdrawn as Saffron had feared and it seemed that Jarvis had done her some good by being with her through the dark hours of the night.

'I feel very down today,' she admitted heavily. 'I don't mean to be sorry for myself but it does seem hard, Saffron.'

'It *is* hard,' Saffron said gently, with understanding and compassion. 'But it will get easier, I promise. I'm not saying that you'll forget. How could you? But remembering will become less painful.'

'Last night . . .' Delia drew a deep breath. 'I'm afraid I upset everyone—Dr Ben, Jarvis, everyone.'

'Has he been reproaching you?' It was quick and indignant.

'No. He was cross with Philip, I know. But he was very kind to me. He *can* be kind.'

'He'll answer to me if he isn't,' Saffron said, in a mockingly stern tone. 'I won't allow him to upset my patient.'

'You're so strong,' Delia said, wonderingly. 'You can stand up to him. You don't know how difficult it is for me.'

'You make him sound like a tyrant!' Saffron laughed, teasing her gently. 'He cares about you, Delia. He won't mind if you say no to him occasionally. After all, you disappointed him once and it wasn't the end of the world!'

'Ivor died.'

It was the merest breath of a reply but the words and their import slammed Saffron's heart with the force of a thunderbolt. She realised with a shock that Delia was crediting Jarvis with god-like powers. Delia was irrationally afraid of the consequences if she should thwart him again!

CHAPTER SIX

DETERMINED to distract her patient from such morbid fears and fancies, Saffron set about encouraging her to get out of her wheelchair.

'Try to walk a few steps today, Delia,' she said briskly. 'You're starting an intensive course of physiotherapy this morning but I'd like you to prove that your treatment at Howlett did help. I'll be right here.' She backed away across the lawn, smiling but firm.

Delia shook her head, her face crumpling. 'It's too soon. I really don't feel like it—not today. I'm tired and I hurt and there doesn't seem to be any point . . .' There was the threat of more tears in the way that her plaintive voice shook and trailed off.

She'd scarcely cried at all throughout the weeks she'd spent at the Howlett Memorial. Returning to Pethnavick seemed to have opened the floodgates, Saffron thought wryly. Tears might wash away some of the hurt. They were also a weakness that she didn't want to encourage.

She went back to her patient, understanding. 'I know. All right—we won't rush matters,' she agreed gently. 'There's plenty of time, of course. I only thought it would please Jarvis to see that you're working at getting well as quickly as possible.' She'd use him if it would help Delia. But by showing him in the role of tender and caring friend rather than despotic lover who wreaked terrible revenge on a woman who dared to defy and disappoint him. She wondered if Jarvis knew how the girl's disturbed mind regarded him and how he felt about it.

'You can't want him to feel that it might have been a
mistake to bring you home. He's so anxious about you,
Delia . . .'

The strategy was absurdly obvious and wouldn't have
fooled a child, but it worked just as she'd known it
would. Delia would do anything to please Jarvis—anything at all! Saffron had supposed that she was anxious to
make up to him for the hurt of jilting him to marry Ivor.
Now she wished that she could believe it was such a
logical and acceptable reason.

Delia struggled bravely to her feet, biting her lip
against the discomfort it caused her convalescent spine,
fighting to overcome the weakness and the lassitude and
the conviction that it didn't much matter if she never
walked again. She managed just three steps before she
gave up on a little sob of despair and almost fell into
Saffron's hovering arms.

Helping her into the wheelchair, Saffron soothed her
with a warm smile, a reassuring touch and sympathetic
words.

'You can do better than that, Delia!'

The deep voice rang out across the terrace. Saffron
turned to shoot an angry glance at the imperious doctor,
wondering just how long he'd been watching and listening from the shadows of Delia's room.

'You're not trying!' It was stern, autocratic.

Delia dissolved into the threatening, too-ready tears.
Jarvis turned away, impatient. Saffron paused only to
thrust a box of tissues into her patient's lap and sped
after the doctor, furious. She caught him just as he
emerged into the corridor.

'Just a minute, Dr Tregarron!'

He turned, a sardonic eyebrow raised. 'Well? What is
it, Nurse?'

'Did you have to interfere at that point? She was

trying, really making an effort! You ask far too much of her. Why must you be so hard, so demanding?'

In the heat of her concern for Delia and her annoyance with him, Saffron quite forgot to be embarrassed by this encounter with the man who'd kissed her beneath the moon at their last meeting. Just then, she was much too angry to be reminded that he'd figured so prominently in her dreams that she'd woken with the thought of him in heart and mind.

'I fear that you're much too soft to do her any good at all,' he countered coldly. 'You must encourage her to keep at it and not to give in, you know. Delia has to get on with the business of living—and being able to walk again is the first step.'

'She doesn't want to get on with a life that no longer seems to hold anything for her,' Saffron reminded him fiercely, astonished by his lack of understanding. 'It's cruel to force the pace before she's ready!'

Jarvis looked at her levelly. 'Cruel to be kind, Nurse Pierce—a nursery expression with a lot of truth in it. Do you really suppose that your soft-pedal approach does any good?'

'I'm certainly not convinced that your bullying methods are the answer!'

His mouth tightened with more than dislike of the accusing words, for at that moment a nurse appeared at the door of a room further along the corridor and glanced in their direction, curious, obviously attracted by the heated exchange. It was unconventional, to say the least, for a nurse to challenge a senior doctor's authority or methods of treatment. It was a new experience for Jarvis to be challenged by anyone, family, friend or employee. This girl did it too often!

'That's enough, Nurse Pierce,' he said, ominously quiet, a nerve jumping in his jaw. 'This is no place for a slanging match. So far I've tolerated your attitude for Delia's sake, but I don't care for it. God knows why, but she's fond of you, depends on you! *That's* why you're here. But my concern for Delia won't extend to putting up indefinitely with anything that you choose to hurl at me. You don't have to like me or my methods. But I do insist on a certain degree of respect from a nurse in my employ!'

Saffron was silenced. Not by the tone or the blaze in the dark eyes. But by her own admission that the rebuke was justified. However she felt, she had no right to challenge him or abuse him so roundly.

'I'm sorry,' she said stiffly.

He inclined his dark head in haughty acceptance of an obviously grudging apology. 'Very well. I know that you are as anxious as we all are about Delia. But you won't do her or yourself a scrap of good by continually crossing swords with me. It must be difficult for you to accept that I do understand what she's going through and that I do know what I'm about. I'm only a mere male, after all,' he finished dryly.

Saffron coloured slightly at the sardonic rider. It was just as though he saw directly into her impatient, scornful thoughts. It was disconcerting that he was so perceptive and it was one more reason to dislike him, she decided defensively. Any man who knew so much about the workings of a woman's mind was too experienced for her liking!

'I must get back to her. Excuse me, Dr Tregarron,' she said abruptly, deliberately formal.

As she turned away, Jarvis detained her with a light hand on her arm. He glanced swiftly up and down the now deserted corridor, the curious nurse having tactfully returned to her patient and closed the door.

'Delia wants us to be friends, you know. You're

making it very hard for me to like you, Saffron.' It was direct but not unfriendly.

Feeling reproached, she took refuge in righteous indignation. 'I suppose you weren't liking me when you kissed me last night!' she exclaimed impulsively, perhaps unwisely, in low and angry tones.

He considered her with a slight smile glinting in his eyes. 'Last night I wanted to make love to a very pretty girl in the moonlight,' he said. 'What has that to do with liking?'

Saffron almost choked on her fury. 'I wish I'd slapped your face!' she said through gritted teeth.

The smile deepened and warmed his handsome face. 'Why—when you enjoyed it just as much as I did!'

Saffron stiffened and shook off the disturbing touch of his hand, infuriated by his arrogance all over again and refusing to admit the attraction of the smile that transformed his rather harsh features. Disdaining to reply, she stalked across Delia's pleasant room to the open french window and the terrace, affront in every line of her slim figure in the pale lilac uniform. She knew that his mocking eyes were on her stiff back and she heard him laugh softly. Fuming, she wondered how he could suppose that they'd ever be anything but sworn enemies!

Delia was on her feet and several determined steps away from her wheelchair when Saffron emerged from the house. She turned a pale but gritty face to her nurse and waved her away firmly.

'I *will* do it,' she said. 'Jarvis is right. I mustn't be defeatist. I owe it to Ivor to get well and get on with living!'

Saffron silently wished that her patient wouldn't quote Jarvis Tregarron at her with every other sentence.

'Well done!' she applauded brightly. 'But you mustn't overdo it. It's going to take a long time and you mustn't allow Jarvis or anyone else to rush you.'

Delia leaned on her heavily as she was helped to the chair, too slight and too frail to be a noticeable weight. 'You were quarrelling with Jarvis. I heard raised voices . . .'

'Quarrelling?' Saffron laughed, shook her head. 'A slight difference of opinion, that's all! I hope I know better than to quarrel with a doctor who also happens to be the boss! I want to keep this job for just as long as you need me.'

'You don't understand him at all, I'm afraid.'

'No, I don't,' Saffron admitted, forbearing to mention that she had no desire to do so. 'I've never met anyone quite like him, to be frank—and I can't pretend to like him. Not even to please you,' she added with a smile and a quick hug for the girl who was her friend as much as her patient.

'I don't want you to like him to please *me*,' Delia returned cryptically. Then, looking beyond Saffron as a tall young man came out to the terrace, she held out a hand in warm welcome. She found a smile for him, too. 'Are you dreadfully in disgrace?' she demanded, warmly sympathetic. 'Poor Philip! Jarvis is so *quick*!'

'But usually right.'

Philip Tregarron smiled at Saffron in a friendly greeting, blithely unaware of how much he irritated her with the generous comment on his cousin. Saffron marvelled at the affection and respect that the man seemed to command from people who had most reason to dislike and despise him, and wondered why everyone was so ready to make allowances for him. The more she knew of Jarvis Tregarron, the less she liked him!

'You survived the stroll in the moonlight with my unpredictable cousin, I see, Nurse,' Philip said to her with slightly strained humour.

Her answering smile held a warning. For she hadn't said anything to Delia about the uncomfortable few hours that she'd spent with the Tregarrons. Tactfully, she left the couple. She had plenty to do and no desire to play gooseberry, she thought dryly. Glancing back, she saw that the surgeon had taken Delia's frail hand into a warm clasp and he was smiling down at her with obvious affection.

'I'm glad that you're feeling so much better this morning,' she heard him say tautly. 'I've been anxious.'

It was obviously an understatement. Philip looked tense and drawn and his words were jerky, betraying a much greater concern for Delia than one would expect from a mere cousin by marriage. She wondered if she was the only person to suspect the dawn of love in Philip's concern for the lovely girl with her burden of sorrow. He seemed to be warm-hearted, gentle and kind and good-natured, very suited to the sensitive Delia. It was much too soon to be thinking of another husband for her, of course. But Saffron felt that Philip Tregarron must be a more suitable choice than the man who'd already cast himself in the role.

Jarvis would crush Delia's sensitive spirit. He needed a wife with a fiery nature to match his own, one who would stand up to him and give back as good as she got and wouldn't be quelled by his arrogant and dominant personality. Such a marriage might be tempestuous and uncertain but it would never be boring . . .

Delia spent much of her morning with the new physiotherapist who took her off for massage, exercises and heat treatment and a session in the hydrotherapy pool. Bronwen was glad to make use of another pair of hands when Saffron declared that she had nothing to do for her particular patient for the time being.

Saffron was adjusting the flow of a drip for a patient

recovering from a hip replacement operation when Tom van Wyk walked into the room.

'Good morning, Nurse.' The consultant's greeting was formal but his smile was warm with approval and admiration. 'How is Mrs Baxter this morning?'

'Sleepy but doing very nicely, sir.' Saffron took the patient's chart from its hook at the foot of the bed and handed it to him.

He glanced through the notes on the chart and then, satisfied, bent over his patient. 'I'm glad to hear that you're doing so well, Mrs Baxter. We shall have you running around in no time,' he promised, raising his voice to penetrate the mists of morphine.

He added a note of his own to the chart while Saffron settled the patient more comfortably and then they left the room together.

'I'm really here to see Mrs Tregarron,' he said as they walked along the corridor. 'How is she?'

Saffron wondered if he'd heard about the upset of the previous evening. He seemed to be a close friend of the family. It would be interesting to know if he'd been in favour of Delia's return to Cornwall or if he shared her own view that it was much too soon.

'She's suffering some reaction from the journey and from meeting the family for the first time since the loss of her husband,' she said carefully. 'She's rather emotional, slightly depressed, and trying very hard to be brave.'

'It's natural that she should be depressed. Poor girl! She has very little to be cheerful about at the moment.' He spoke with a warm compassion that instantly endeared him to Saffron. 'But there doesn't seem to be any reason why she shouldn't make a full recovery, physically, at least. I've seen the X-rays and read the reports from the Howlett Memorial and there don't appear to be any complications. The damaged nerves are healing and it's simply a matter of time—and mental attitude, of course. The last is particularly important.'

'I agree with you, sir,' Saffron said firmly.

The consultant paused by one of the long windows and looked down at her with a friendly interest in his blue eyes. 'I gather that she's come to depend on you to a very great extent, so it's particularly fortunate that you were able to travel with her at such short notice. I believe that you're a Kit's nurse, by the way? Meredith—I mean Mrs Clay Tregarron, of course—will welcome you with open arms. But perhaps you already know each other from your training days?'

'Apparently we missed each other by a few months. She was in the set before me.' Saffron smiled at him, liking the warm and easy manner that was so different to the chilly arrogance of his colleague and which made her feel like a junior nurse at times. 'But we met last night and discovered some mutual friends.' If he'd heard about that disastrous evening then he obviously hadn't heard it from Meredith, she decided.

'She's a charming woman and an excellent theatre sister,' he commended. 'Do you have any experience of theatre work?'

'I did six months as staff nurse in Theatre before leaving Kit's,' she told him. 'I thought it might be useful experience and I'd enjoyed my spell of theatre work during training.'

'Then you'll certainly be called on to help out if Meredith is short of staff at any time.'

'I hope so. Delia won't need full-time nursing and I like to be busy.'

'Oh, you'll be busy—one way or another,' he promised, twinkling. 'Meredith will be delighted to have a pair of experienced hands at her beck and call. You'll find her a good friend, by the way—and, being new to everyone and everything, you'll need friends.' He smiled suddenly. 'Which reminds me that we have a date for a cream tea. You haven't forgotten?' It was low, conspiratorial, as a nurse came out of the clinical room just along the corridor, pushing a trolley that was laid in readiness for the dressings round.

'No, sir. I'm keeping it in mind,' Saffron said demurely, hands clasped behind her back like a dutiful nurse receiving instructions from a doctor while a smile danced in her grey eyes.

'Good . . .' Tom waited until the nurse had passed them without even a glance, for they were apparently in earnest discussion of a patient. 'I'm staking my claim before half the bachelors in Cornwall get to hear about the pretty new nurse at the Tregarron Clinic,' he went on lightly. 'When shall we meet? When will you be free?'

'Would Sunday suit you?' It had pleased Saffron to learn that she would have every weekend off duty rather than odd days at intervals. Nurses seldom found it so easy to organise a social life!

'Perfectly. We'll make a day of it, I think—lunch as well as tea. Then we'll have time to visit a few of the beauty spots. Eleven o'clock?'

Having secured her promise that she would be waiting for him at the appointed time, Tom van Wyk went away to find out how Delia was responding to the urgings of the new physiotherapist. Saffron turned to find Bronwen regarding her from the door of the clinical room, kindly amusement in her warm brown eyes. She obviously knew exactly what had been going on between her and the blond consultant.

'Made a conquest, is it?' she teased gently.

Saffron laughed. 'I don't know about that! But he seems rather nice. I hope you aren't about to warn me that he's the worst rake in the district!'

'No, no.' Bronwen was reassuring. 'He likes the girls, mind. But there's no harm in him that I've ever heard. Careful of his reputation like every doctor, see. He always says that he's looking for a wife—and enjoying himself while he looks.'

'Then perhaps we can help each other,' Saffron said promply, mischief gleaming in the grey eyes. 'I'm looking for a husband, and he's just my type! Tall, fair and handsome—and a professional man, to boot! What more could any nurse want?' It was light, laughing banter that no one could possibly take seriously.

'Is it possible that you have Miss Foster's X-rays on your desk instead of in her file where they should be, Sister?' Jarvis Tregarron's harsh tones cut across the conversation as he suddenly emerged from a room on the other side of the corridor. 'If so, I should like them. And may I suggest that you lower your voices if you must discuss your personal concerns in corridors. It may entertain the patients but it also convinces them that you have time on your hands which might be better spent in attending to their needs!'

Saffron hadn't known that he was still on the ward. Meeting the dark eyes, she found them hard and indifferent. So it was foolish to fancy that it had been her light-hearted remarks that had irritated him. He was merely annoyed that two supposedly busy nurses could find time to gossip about Tom van Wyk. Quite rightly, she admitted fairly. Paying patients could be very sharp-tongued about nurses who didn't come running as soon as a buzzer was pressed, however busy they might in fact be, or non-urgent the need.

'Miss Foster's X-rays? I believe I do have them, Doctor. I'll get them right away!' Bronwen bustled away in the direction of her office, skirts rustling, bright patches of colour flying in her rounded cheeks at the dry rebuke.

Saffron was made of sterner stuff. She neither flushed nor fled. Jarvis looked at her with a frown. She was threatening to become a thorn in his side, he thought impatiently.

'Nothing to do, Nurse Pierce?' he demanded. 'This must seem like a holiday camp after the Howlett Memorial. But the first rule here is that our nurses should always appear to be usefully occupied.' It was cool, cutting.

Saffron's eyes sparked with annoyance. 'Oh? I thought it was always to remember that you're king of the castle,' she said tartly.

His dark brows snapped together suddenly. 'Like it or not, I *am* king of this particular castle—and it will be wise for you to remember it,' he told her grimly. 'For if you speak to me like that just once in front of a patient or another nurse, you're out! I'll sack you on the spot, Delia or no Delia!'

'May I suggest that you lower your voice?' she said sweetly, refusing to admit to a flicker of dismay at the threat—and not entirely because she'd promised to see Delia through her convalescence. 'Why should we entertain the patients with our quarrel?'

As if to support her warning that they could be overheard, a blue light flashed on and off above a door at the end of the corridor. Jarvis glanced at it impatiently.

'Attend to that, Nurse!' he said dismissively, with just that high-handed note in his deep voice that instinctively set her fuming.

He was undeniably the kingpin of the Tregarron Clinic while she was just a nurse. But she'd usually met with courtesy and even friendliness from the crustiest of consultants or most distinguished of medical men at

Kit's and other hospitals. So she resented his dislike and his complete failure to conceal it.

He might make her fume but Saffron was too well-trained and too conscientious to ignore a patient's summons or a doctor's instructions. So, seething but dutiful, she hurried to his bidding, leaving their quarrel in mid-air.

Somehow it seemed inevitable that it would be picked up and carried on at their next meeting. Come what may, it seemed that they couldn't simply ignore each other—although it would be much more comfortable if they could, Saffron thought crossly . . .

CHAPTER SEVEN

SAFFRON quickly settled down to the new job and new surroundings and new people and felt that she could be happy working at the Tregarron Clinic. The only fly in the ointment was Jarvis Tregarron and, rather than clash with him continually, she kept out of his way as much as possible in the next few days. They would never agree, she felt. They would never like each other. So it was wise to look on him as doctor and employer who would never be a friend.

But she was becoming anxious about Delia and wondered if she could keep her tongue between her teeth for much longer. Her patient returned from lengthy sessions with the clever but demanding Ingrid Jensen, tired and drained of the little energy that she had left to her of late. Saffron couldn't feel that it was doing her any good to work so hard at getting well.

After one session that had taken up the entire morning, she was so wan and exhausted and painwracked that Saffron felt far too much was being demanded of her— and said so with her usual impulsive candour as she helped her weary patient into bed.

Delia managed a small smile as she sank against the pillows. 'You worry too much about me. Jarvis won't allow me to overdo things,' she said with touching confidence in his concern.

Saffron's lips tightened ominously. She punched up a pillow as if she wished that the doctor was on the receiving end of the blows. 'Jarvis seems to be leaving you entirely to the tender mercies of Miss Jensen.'

'He says that the programme has been carefully worked out so that I'll feel like doing a little more each day and gradually grow stronger,' Delia went on serenely. 'Ingrid's had marvellous results with other cases like mine and Jarvis says I can cope with it. I expect he's right.'

Too many people had listened and agreed to all that Jarvis Tregarron thought and said for too many years, Saffron decided impatiently. No wonder he was so arrogant, so full of his own importance, so sweepingly convinced that he was always right. There were far too many Delias hanging on his every word and panting for his approval, apparently too timid to argue or question his high-handed dictates. Well, *she* wasn't one of them!

'Jarvis seems to be expecting a miracle,' she said sharply, not at all surprised to find that her patient's pulse was much too rapid and that she had a slight temperature and no appetite for her lunch.

Leaving Delia to rest, she went to make her report and a strong complaint. She tracked Jarvis to his office where he was talking to a colleague on the house telephone. She paused by the open door, a militant light in her grey eyes, and he glanced at her with a quizzical lift of his eyebrow. Then he motioned to her to enter and wait.

Saffron walked into the room and stood in front of his desk, fury mounting by the moment as his dark eyes seemed to rest speculatively on her slender figure while he continued his conversation with the disembodied voice on the end of the telephone wire.

He kept her waiting for some moments. Then he rang off and leaned back in his chair to look at her thoughtfully.

'Too much for her, was it?' He neatly took the wind out of her sails with the smooth words. 'I thought it might be. But I'm told that physiotherapy of that nature needs to be continuous and consistent to do any good.'

'Well, it isn't doing Delia much good at the moment,' Saffron said hotly. 'She's on the point of collapse!'

Jarvis smiled slightly. 'Oh, come now! Is it possible that you're guilty of a slight exaggeration, Nurse Pierce?' he drawled.

She was, of course. Two spots of angry colour flew into her cheeks. 'She's certainly far from well, anyway,' she said stonily, defending her unprofessional lapse. 'I'm very concerned for my patient, Dr Tregarron.'

'She's tired, naturally. That was only to be expected from such an intensive course.' He glanced at his watch. 'I do have an appointment,' he said carelessly. 'Perhaps you could get to the point?'

Saffron bristled with sudden indignation. 'If you'd nursed her through the last six weeks, you might have some idea of just how much she can handle and the likely rate of her progress in the next six weeks! But you didn't bother to ask the opinion of the one person who might be expected to help with the planning of any programme of treatment for her patient!'

It rankled that he hadn't wanted her to sit in on that conference with Tom van Wyk and hadn't suggested that she might be present when he discussed Delia's condition with the Swedish girl.

'Sit down,' Jarvis said sharply, peremptorily.

Startled, Saffron sank into a chair. But she looked at him with a challenge in her grey eyes.

Jarvis reached for a pencil and began to turn it between his strong fingers, studying it thoughtfully while he marshalled his words. There was no reason why he should explain or defend himself to this militant young woman who was so determined to dislike him. But perhaps it was time to set the record straight on one or two points.

'I didn't travel all the way to London week after week merely for the pleasure of seeing Delia,' he said carefully. 'I followed her progress with great concern and took the trouble to consult everyone connected with her case. The surgeon who operated, the doctors who attended her, the sister in charge, the physiotherapist who'd already begun the difficult task of restoring her mobility and the psychiatrist who had long talks with her on several occasions to ascertain her mental state. Also, I discussed her condition with Tom van Wyk, who is probably the best orthopaedic surgeon in the West Country. There didn't seem to be any need to consult *you*, but you must forgive me if I've dented your dignity. You see, I knew that you would quickly put me right if my ideas for the best possible treatment for Delia didn't coincide with yours,' he finished very dryly.

The sardonic words and tone made Saffron feel foolish. And it had been foolish to suppose that he wouldn't do exactly as he said before he took over the responsibility for Delia's welfare. He was not simply the man who loved her. He was also a caring and conscientious doctor. Like him or not, she had to admit that after just a few days of working with him.

She was silent, arms folded tightly across her breasts, a chastened expression in her grey eyes. She had been guilty of arrogance just as insufferable as his own—and with much less cause, she thought wryly.

Jarvis studied the suddenly subdued girl with her smooth auburn hair and pretty face and warmly impulsive nature that caught at his heart against his will. 'I wonder why you feel that you're the only person who really cares about Delia,' he said gently.

Saffron's heart bumped in her breast as she heard the softening of his voice, the unexpected tenderness that seemed to speak of his love for the beautiful and tragic girl.

'I know you care,' she said quietly, defensively. 'I'm not belittling your concern or doubting how you feel about Delia. It means far too much to her.'

'I believe it does,' he agreed. 'Responsibility for her decisions has always been hard for Delia to shoulder. She cannot bear to feel that she isn't much-loved or instantly forgiven, no matter what she says or does. It would be cruel for me to behave as though I don't care at this particular time, don't you think?'

Saffron looked at him, startled, unsure. '*Isn't* she forgiven?' The quick words betrayed that she knew all about his shattered hopes, if not the full details of how and why and when.

He regarded her, dark eyes intent. 'Do you think I'm the kind to forgive and forget so easily?'

'No,' she said bluntly, frowning. 'I've never thought that about you . . .'

Unexpectedly, a smile flickered about the sensual mouth. 'I can always rely on you to be brutally honest,' he said, amused. 'However, you're right, of course. I *haven't* forgiven Delia. But I care enough to compromise my pride to some extent. You may believe that it isn't easy for a Tregarron!'

Saffron felt that he had forgiven whether he was prepared to admit it or not. It was obvious that he loved too much to let even his stiff-necked pride stand in the way of the happiness that he still hoped to find with Delia. Something twisted suddenly in her breast. Almost a pain.

She didn't like him but she could feel compassion for a proud man who'd been hurt and humiliated by the woman he loved and his own brother, she decided. No one could doubt that it had hit him hard. There was evidence of it in the dark eyes, the tension of his powerful frame, the way that a pulse throbbed heavily in his temple.

'I don't know why I assumed that you didn't know,' he said abruptly, almost impatiently. 'There are enough people to tell the story of the bride who went to her wedding with a different groom at almost the last moment.'

Saffron's grey eyes widened. The anger and taut humiliation behind the words was shocking. So was their implication. 'I never heard what happened . . .'

'Delia didn't tell you? Well, no, perhaps she wouldn't,' he conceded dryly. 'It shows her in a poorer light than she would probably wish you to see her.'

'There's no need for you to tell me, either,' Saffron said quickly.

His gaze softened slightly. 'Nice of you to be concerned for my pride. But I think it can stand the strain,' he said coolly. 'You obviously know that Delia had agreed to marry me? Everything was arranged. The day, the church, the reception, even the honeymoon. Delia changed nothing but the bridegroom—and he had the same surname to round things off nicely!'

Saffron stared, appalled. 'But that's dreadful!'

He shrugged. 'She couldn't see why she shouldn't go ahead with a wedding that she'd planned so carefully over a period of several months,' he explained with a wry smile.

'I can't believe that anyone could be so insensitive!'

'Nor could I believe it,' he told her grimly. 'But that's the way it happened.'

Saffron was dumbfounded. It didn't seem to tally with what she knew of Delia, even if she had only known her for a few short weeks and not in the best of circumstances. 'I just don't understand.'

'She didn't want to wait. She'd tumbled into love with Ivor and new arrangements would take time—and where was the need when the same guests would be invited and the wedding held in the same church? Fortunately, she drew the line at suggesting that I should take Ivor's place as best man!'

'But your brother! Surely he . . .' Saffron broke off. Even the merest hint of criticism of the dead Ivor must seem tasteless to the brother who mourned him, she thought ruefully.

'Delia can be very persuasive. And perhaps I didn't protest loudly enough. Somehow, she assumed that I didn't mind what she did as long as she was happy. It's all so unimportant now, of course. It doesn't really matter any more why or where or when. She wanted Ivor—and she married him.'

'And hurt you badly in the process!' Saffron said quickly, indignant on his behalf.

Anyone could have a change of heart. She didn't blame Delia for that and no doubt it hadn't been easy for her to admit it to a man like Jarvis Tregarron. But to have so little thought for his feelings—or his pride! That was unforgivable.

But he had forgiven. He loved her that much. Delia was luckier than she really deserved to be, Saffron thought hotly, momentarily forgetting the tragedy that had plunged a bride into widowhood within hours of her wedding.

She saw the shutters come down abruptly at her impulsive words. She'd made the mistake of being sorry for him and showing it, she realised. His pride might have been trampled in the dust but it still survived, fiercer than ever.

'At least she made a decision for herself, probably for the first and last time in her life,' he said coolly. 'As it had such tragic results it's unlikely that she'll ever make another if she can help it.' He rose and went to the door, opened it wide. 'I think we must both have urgent claims on our time, Nurse Pierce.'

It was so dismissive that Saffron had no choice but to walk from his office, feeling that he'd instantly regretted that brief relaxation of his reserve. But she'd been given a glimpse of the very private man behind the arrogant and chilling mask, and it had improved her understanding, if not her liking, of him.

He was still her least favourite man of all time, she told herself firmly . . .

Except perhaps for his cousin Clay, Saffron amended later that day, finding herself cornered in the clinical room by the surgeon who was determined to exhibit his ardent interest in her before he'd let her escape.

Saffron counted sterile suture packs as though her life depended on it while he watched her with dark eyes, so like his cousin's, stripping her naked with the speculative gleam in their depths. He was so obviously in hot pursuit that she suspected he looked on all women as fair game, and herself as a willing victim. Her irritation with Jarvis earlier in the week had led her to smile rather too warmly on Clay Tregarron—and this was the result, she thought ruefully.

'You're very efficient,' he said admiringly.

'Anyone can count,' she returned lightly.

'And you aren't easily distracted from your counting?'

'I'm used to being watched while I work. Isn't every nurse?'

'That isn't what I meant—and you know it,' he said softly, reproachfully. 'I must be losing my touch if you won't neglect a routine chore to give me five minutes of your time.'

'It isn't *my* time,' she pointed out firmly. 'I'm on duty

until four.' As soon as she'd said the words, she realised her mistake. For he instantly assumed that she was merely being discreet—and giving him a hefty hint into the bargain.

He looked at the wall clock, comparing it with his watch. 'Another twenty minutes. You're right to remind me that we shall need to be careful. There are eyes and ears everywhere in this place! Have you explored the copse yet? I usually walk my dog in that direction every day about four-thirty . . .' He smiled at her meaningfully.

Saffron made a mental note to avoid that part of the grounds at all costs. Clay Tregarron *and* a secluded copse? No way! She'd be much too busy fighting for her honour to admire the greenery!

'I'm afraid you aren't getting the message, Mr Tregarron,' she said firmly. 'If I've said or done anything to encourage you then I'm very sorry. But I don't play those kind of games with married men.'

The last words were another mistake, she realised ruefully. For he smiled at her so reassuringly that she knew he thought that she objected to his marital status rather than his personal charms. He was so conceited that he believed himself to be irresistible to women, she thought impatiently.

'Meredith and I have an understanding about these things,' he said airily. 'What makes you so sure that it's a game, anyway?'

Saffron shot a glance at the persistent surgeon, half-amused, half-exasperated. 'It isn't likely to be anything else!'

'Don't be so sure, sweetheart. You're on my mind, night and day. You're the loveliest girl I've seen in a very long time. You wouldn't believe what it does to my blood pressure just looking at you,' he said softly.

'Then I must be a danger to your health. So stop looking!' She guessed that, like his cousin, Clay Tregarron didn't care to be thwarted. But he lacked his cousin's magnetism, even if he had an equal share of the Tregarron good looks. More to the point, he was married and ought not to be in pursuit of her and she felt sorry for Meredith, who must be aware of her husband's amorous inclinations.

'More of a danger to my heart, darling.'

'You *are* a practised Casanova,' she said lightly, laughing at him. Nothing dampened a man's ardour like laughter, she'd learned—and he was no exception. But he lacked a sense of humour, she felt, seeing the sudden scowl in his dark eyes. Jarvis would have laughed with her at the exchange of absurdities, she thought suddenly, inconsequentially.

'You could try taking me seriously.' A hint of annoyance and frustration throbbed in the velvet voice.

'You've no right to be serious about me,' she told him levelly. 'And I don't see how you can be when we only met for the first time a few days ago!'

'How long does it take to fall in love?' he returned promptly, predictably.

'I don't know. Do you?' Saffron countered sweetly. She moved away from him to open a drawer that contained an array of shining surgical instruments in transparent sterile packs and checked their contents with an experienced eye. 'Perhaps it's a habit with you.'

Clay came up behind her and she felt the touch of his fingers on the back of her neck in confident caress. She jerked her head away.

'Such a lovely face,' he said quietly. 'And such a sharp tongue . . .' He stooped to kiss the slender lines of her neck.

'And an even sharper scalpel right to hand,' she

warned swiftly, thrusting him away with a militant sparkle in her eyes and a flush of indignation in her small face. 'I'm not playing hard to get. I'm not interested! Do you want it in writing?'

Clay looked down at the furious face, the rigid figure, and reluctantly admitted defeat for the moment. She was much too attractive for him to give up all hope of wearing down her resistance in time. 'Pity. We could have made beautiful music together. Let me know if you change your mind.'

'I'll send you a message via Meredith,' she told him brightly.

The door closed on him with a decidedly irritated click. Saffron was still seething when Bronwen opened it a few moments later and came into the clinical room. The Welsh girl smiled at her in sympathetic understanding, having seen the surgeon on his way from the ward in obviously disgruntled mood.

'Wolf at the door, is it?' she suggested lightly.

'Something like that.' Saffron smiled. 'It's silly to let him get under my skin, I know. I've met plenty like him since I came into nursing.'

'I meant to warn you about our Dr Clay but I dare say you handled his old nonsense without any help from me. There's nothing like a hospital training to teach a girl how to take care of herself, is there? Particularly working on male wards! I've always said that the first sign that a patient is over the worst is when he lifts his head from the pillow to watch a pretty nurse walk down the ward!'

'And the second is when he gets out of bed to follow her!' Saffron laughed, her irritation with Clay Tregarron receding rapidly before Bronwen's common-sense reminder that amorous advances were an occupational hazard for many nurses. 'I didn't have too much trouble with the patients, actually. But some medical students were a nuisance, lying in wait in quiet corridors or convenient linen cupboards to snatch a kiss when Sister wasn't looking.'

'Always the ones you didn't fancy, too,' Bronwen sympathised, brown eyes twinkling.

'True! The ones I did usually had their eye on someone else! It's a hard life for a poor nurse in search of a doctor to marry.' Saffron heaved a mock sigh.

They joked, but nursing wasn't all fun and flirtation for a student nurse. It was long hours of hard work on the wards and poring over books and worrying about exams in off-duty hours. It was chivvying ward sisters and scolding staff nurses and demanding patients who expected her to be a *real* nurse, unaware that the stripes on her cap indicated degrees of ignorance rather than ability! It was never-ending rounds, perpetual weariness, aching feet and backs, always being rushed and never having enough time for the hundred and one chores expected of a junior nurse.

In the first year, there was the constant dread, reinforced by irate ward sisters and impatient senior nurses, that the coveted silver badge of a state registered nurse might never be won.

In the second year, life became a little easier and a student nurse began to feel that she might not be such a handicap to Sister or such a nuisance to busy staff nurses or such a menace to helpless and unsuspecting patients. No longer the awkward and ignorant junior who did more than her fair share of dirty jobs on the ward, she found that she was expected to train the first-years in her turn and it seemed that she was nearer to becoming a real nurse than she'd known.

In the third year, finals loomed—but she was kept much too busy being a real nurse on the ward or in theatre to worry about success or failure. The growing confidence of Sister and staff nurses and the touching trust of patients in her experience and efficiency made her feel that the shining silver badge might be pinned to her breast at the end of her training, after all.

Saffron had never regretted becoming a nurse. She had found too many rewards for all the hard work and necessary dedication and she felt that she was privileged to belong to a respected and highly-valued profession.

As the two girls went off duty, Bronwen reverted to the subject of Clay Tregarron. 'You don't want to worry if he doesn't give up too easily. It's just a lot of talk with him, see. No one takes him seriously.'

'Least of all me!' Saffron declared.

Bronwen glanced at her with a teasing smile. 'Not your type, then. Like them blond, do you? Tall, fair and handsome like a consultant who shall remain nameless! Dark men are two a penny in this part of the world, after all.'

'And too many of them are Tregarrons,' Saffron said with feeling as they emerged into the sunshine of yet another glorious day.

She didn't mind the gentle teasing. Tom van Wyk had made no secret of his admiration or his invitation and they were both free agents. But she did wonder if Bronwen was slightly envious. The Welsh girl seemed to be content with her rugger-playing boyfriend but there was a wistfulness in the warm brown eyes whenever the consultant was mentioned.

Saffron liked Tom and she was looking forward to the day that she'd promised to spend with him. But she didn't like him so much that she wouldn't gladly give him up to Bronwen if her warm-hearted new friend wanted him.

For, deep down, she knew that she preferred dark men to fair—and one dark man in particular threatened to play havoc with her heart, even though it rebelled at the very suggestion that she could be falling in love with an arrogant, unfeeling doctor who was deeply in love with another woman . . .

CHAPTER EIGHT

HAVING changed from her uniform into a cool cheese-cloth shirt that was almost the same faded blue as her jeans, Saffron strolled across the cliff meadow on her way to the beach. It was the end of another day of feeling that she was being paid far too much to do too little. She liked to be busy. She was used to a much faster pace of working and many more demands made upon her nursing skills.

There seemed to be very little nursing involved in looking after the convalescent Delia, and the clinic certainly wasn't short of trained staff. Saffron suspected that a job had been found for her just to please Delia's invalid fancy and, foolish though it might be, she felt that she was under some kind of an obligation to Jarvis Tregarron as a result. She didn't like that.

He needn't expect her to be grateful, she thought with pride, pausing at the top of the steep path that led down to the beach. She was a good nurse and she'd left a good job at the Howlett Memorial because she'd believed that Delia needed her. It was becoming increasingly obvious that Delia didn't need her at all, she thought wryly. Not while she had Jarvis on one hand and a tenderly devoted and very attentive Philip on the other!

Saffron looked down at the deserted beach. All the week, frequent and tantalising glimpses of the sea's sparkling, foam-crested surface and the clusters of craggy rocks on the skyline had been drawing her like a magnet. She made her way carefully down the path that seemed to be crumbling in places and crossed the secluded beach with its clean, silvery sand and tempting little hollows among the rocks.

Sand, sea, sunshine and the rugged beauty of the Cornish coast. Inevitably, there had to be a serpent in this Garden of Eden! But even the thought of Jarvis Tregarron couldn't dim her delight in her surroundings as she settled down to enjoy the solitude.

Everyone else was being very kind and friendly towards a 'foreigner'—and that made it easier for her to overlook one man's coolness and another's too-obvious admiration. Philip made up for the pair of them! The more she knew of the young surgeon with his sweet smile and warm friendliness and the gentle courtesy that reminded her of Dr Ben, the more she liked him.

When Saffron liked someone she allowed it to show, and so it probably wasn't surprising that a few tongues had wagged about Philip's frequent visits to the orthopaedic ward that week. Delia was the magnet, of course. But it seemed that Philip didn't mind the grapevine's suggestions that he was interested in the new nurse. Delia was far from ready to know that he was patiently waiting in the wings for the day when she might allow him to play a more important role in her life than that of friend and comforter, of course.

Saffron wondered why Philip didn't know that his cousin would never allow another man to come between him and his happiness. Not again . . .

She was drowsing with head on her folded arms when something—maybe a sound or maybe simply animal awareness of another person's presence—made her stir and glance up at the man who'd joined her on the quiet beach.

Earlier, she'd noticed the small dinghy that was tied to a mooring ring, higher up the beach. About a hundred yards out from the shore a cabin cruiser lay at anchor, riding the waves. Saffron had admired its sleek lines and gleaming new paint and felt a flicker of curiosity about its owner.

Now she saw Jarvis bending over the dinghy, storing a bundle aboard. He was wearing only a brief pair of denim shorts and leather sandals and a heavy gold medallion that swung about his neck as he stooped. Saffron was so used to seeing him in formal suit or professional white coat that she was startled to realise his tanned and muscular masculinity.

Watching him as he wound a thick rope about his hands and prepared to drag the dinghy across the beach, she suddenly knew a tingling excitement, a tug of desire for a very attractive man. She'd talked lightly and dismissively of the dangers of physical attraction in the past, never having known its potency for herself and inclined to wonder at those who fell victim to it too easily. Now, she was discovering with dismay that it could be a very dangerous and powerful force.

Jarvis glanced in her direction with a cool nod that told Saffron that he'd been aware of her since he came down to the beach. She rolled over and sat up, surprised to find that the breeze had freshened while she lay in her protected hollow. It cooled the evening and tugged capriciously at her hair and shirt.

He paused when he was a few feet away from where she sat and she wondered if he'd taken her movement for an invitation to stop and speak. Feeling absurdly shy because of thoughts and feelings that he stirred so unexpectedly, she reached for her sandals and slipped them on to her bare feet, getting ready to leave the beach.

Jarvis took in every detail of the gleaming curls that danced on her shoulders, the curve of small breasts outlined by the thin cheesecloth as the wind whipped it

about her body, the youthful look of the casual clothes—
and the hint of challenge in the clear grey eyes and tilted
chin and very pretty face as she turned her head towards
him.

'Don't get caught by the tide, Miss Pierce.' He ges-
tured to the swiftly-flowing water that steadily surged
higher on the beach. 'This is a treacherous part of the
coast.'

'I'm just leaving . . .' Saffron wondered if she had
been too abrupt in reply to a well-meant warning and she
added in friendlier tones, 'Is that your boat out there?'

'It is.'

'Very nice,' she approved.

He regarded her thoughtfully. 'Know anything about
boats?'

'Only enough not to capsize them.' Saffron almost
smiled as she spoke. 'Do you use it for fishing?'

'More as an escape from my too-demanding family,
incessantly ringing telephones, peevish patients—and
nurses who think they can say what they like to me,' he
added with the dawn of a twinkle in the dark eyes.

Saffron looked at him quickly, then looked away. 'As
if you care about that!' she countered, taking the challenge to herself as he'd intended. She reached for a
handful of sand and watched it trickle through her
fingers rather than meet the disturbing glow in his eyes.
Occasionally, fleetingly, she found something to like in
him and resisted the discovery with an instinctive reluctance to become involved in any way with someone
already committed to another woman.

'I don't *like* it,' he said dryly.

'Naturally. It seems to me that no one ever dares to
say anything to you that you might not like,' she returned scornfully, whipping up a dislike that seemed to
be slipping away quite inexplicably. 'I've never known

anyone so spoiled—or so sure of himself! You seem to be regarded as some sort of a god. Everyone's afraid of offending you!'

Jarvis leaned against the dinghy, folding strong arms across his bare chest, surveying her with a mixture of amusement and annoyance. 'Except you.'

'Except me,' she agreed quickly. *She* wasn't afraid of him! A little alarmed by the strange feelings he evoked, perhaps. With the setting sun creating an aureole for his handsome head, warming the strong cast of his features to a sensual beauty and falling across the bronzed and powerful torso, he looked rather like a god. A pagan god who roused all the most primitive emotions in a woman's breast.

'And it's your mission in life to tell me all my faults? For a stranger, you know me too well.'

Saffron was jolted by the dry reminder that they hardly knew each other. There was nothing like a quarrel or two to breed a kind of intimacy, she felt.

'I've heard a lot about you from Delia.'

He raised a sardonic eyebrow. '*Delia* catalogued my faults? It doesn't seem very likely,' he drawled. 'I wonder if she didn't sing my praises so long and so often that you took a dislike to me out of sheer perversity.'

'You are the most conceited . . . !' Saffron broke off. He already knew what she thought of him, and didn't give a damn, she thought crossly.

She sprang to her feet, brushing the sand from her jeans. Conscious that his gaze swept over the lines of her slender figure with very male interest, she wouldn't look at him. She wished that he would take himself off to his boat and sail for some distant shore so that she need never see him again!

He allowed her to turn and walk a few feet before he spoke. 'Like to come on board?' She looked back at him in surprise at the unexpected invitation, and he laughed softly. 'Perhaps you don't trust me? Do you think I mean to throw you to the sharks?'

His smile was disarming, so warm and so enchanting that it took her heart and senses by surprise. Saffron was angry with herself for reacting to a charm that had probably captivated too many women. 'I think you might be tempted!' she retorted.

'Yes. I might well be tempted,' he admitted, a glow of amusement and admiration in his dark eyes.

The way he looked and spoke left her in no doubt that he had a different kind of temptation in mind. Her heart tilted as she met the meaningful warmth in his eyes and she felt a foolish longing to bridge the gulf between them by melting into arms that seemed to want to hold her.

What has liking to do with physical attraction? he'd asked, and Saffron was ready to admit the truth of the words. She didn't like Jarvis Tregarron but his undeniable impact on her emotions caused her to ache for his embrace and long to be swept by his ardent love-making to the towering peaks of ecstasy.

Struggling with the dangerous desire for a too-attractive man, she shook her head, not even trusting herself to smile at him.

'Not a good idea, Dr Tregarron,' she returned coolly. 'If we got to quarrelling again I'd probably push you over the side!'

He shrugged indifferently. 'Just as you like.'

He turned away from her and began to drag the dinghy further down the beach towards the sea. Saffron hadn't expected such a proud man to try persuasion, but she felt slightly let down that he'd accepted her refusal so promptly. Perhaps he had immediately regretted such an impulsive invitation . . .

She made her way across the sand towards the cliff path as Jarvis pushed the dinghy out beyond the shallows and swung himself into it. Saffron glanced over her shoulder as he reached for the oars.

Pausing half-way on the steep climb, she saw that he was rowing strongly towards the anchored boat. She watched the clean sweep of the oars as they swathed through the water in response to his skilled and powerful strokes. He was the kind of man who no doubt did everything well, she thought inconsequentially. Making expert and sensual love to a woman was probably only one of his many accomplishments, for instance.

Reaching the top of the cliff, slightly breathless from the climb, Saffron paused and glanced again to see that Jarvis had reached the small cabin cruiser. She watched him mount the ladder and swing himself to the deck. He secured the dinghy and then straightened, tall and impressive and very masculine even from that distance.

Then he glanced in her direction. Realising that she must be distinctively etched against the skyline, she hastily turned to make her way across the meadow to the dower house. She didn't want him to know that she'd been watching so intently. It would never do for Jarvis Tregarron to suspect her reluctant but growing interest in him.

The next morning, Saffron woke to a fine drizzle of rain. She threw back the covers and padded on bare feet to look at the expanse of leaden sky and the turbulent swell of the sea, hoping that the weather would clear before she set off to meet Bronwen for a day of shopping and exploration before the rugger club dance.

The Welsh girl's friendship, Tom Van Wyk's flattering interest and the easy acceptance of almost everyone she'd met since her arrival in Pethnavick were only a few of the many good things about her new job, she decided, as she stepped out of the shower and wrapped her glowing body in a thick towel, then reached for another to rub at her damp hair.

Delia was making steady progress, even if she was still a long way from full health, and Saffron was almost ready to admit that Jarvis had been right in his decision to bring her back to Cornwall. But she doubted if he'd known that Philip would play so big a part in the process of healing.

Saffron was sure that Philip's unspoken love and concern, which asked so little in return, must do more for Delia than mourning the past or shrinking from the future—or striving to meet the demands that Jarvis was already making on her.

To please Jarvis, Delia worked hard with her physiotherapist and grew stronger every day, although she was still prey to depression and a despair that she did her best to conceal from him. To please him, she talked courageously of soon being well enough to help with the clinic and look after the failing Dr Ben and take her place in the bosom of the family. But Saffron knew that she dreaded the day when she would finally have to accept all the apparently attendant obligations of being a Tregarron.

Delia was so concerned with pleasing him that Saffron wondered if she had mistaken her feelings and married the wrong Tregarron, after all. Jarvis was harsh and ruthless and dominant, but he was a very attractive man with a strength of character and a compelling personality that a woman like Delia might admire. Strong-minded and strong-willed, he was a rock of a man, and no doubt that appealed to the weak and gentle Delia who seemed to need constant support to survive in a cruel world. It was more than likely that she would eventually marry him, Saffron felt.

He would be wasted on Delia. The thought leaped into Saffron's mind and was accompanied by a sickening dismay at the realisation that she was fiercely jealous of his feelings for Delia—feelings that seemed to have survived the worst possible blows to his heart and pride.

Jarvis had kissed her beneath the moon. He'd looked at her with that little glow of desire in his dark eyes and invited her aboard his boat. The chemistry that sparked them both to quick anger also sparked an equally quick reaction to each other's sexuality.

But only a fool would suppose that the way he seemed to feel about her had anything to do with loving—or even liking, she told herself heavily . . .

The rain had stopped but the sky lowered with the threat of more to come when Saffron reached the bus stop opposite the tall and distinctive gates that led to the Tregarron Clinic. She was beginning to realise the benefits of a car of her own after waiting some minutes without a sign of the expected bus for Helston.

A dark blue Jaguar turned out of the gates and headed in her direction. It came to an abrupt halt, with a squeal of brakes, as the driver recognised the identity of the girl in the white raincoat, who was hopefully scanning the distant road.

Jarvis wound down the passenger window and leaned across to speak to her. 'Going to Helston?'

'Me?' Foolishly, Saffron spoke as if she wasn't the only person waiting at the bus stop. 'Yes, I am, actually . . .' It was reluctant admission. With her heart still throbbing from the discovery that he was becoming too important to her, she hadn't wanted to meet him again just yet.

He opened the door. 'Get in.' She hesitated, reacting with fierce independence to the arrogant and authoritative tone. 'Come on!' It was an impatient snap, accompanied by an impatient thrum of the car's powerful engine as his foot hovered on the accelerator.

With a wry glance for the green bus that had finally loomed into view in the distance, Saffron got in beside him. The car shot away from the kerb before she was properly settled in her seat.

'You're in a hurry,' she said with icy sweetness, clutching at her dignity as well as the seat-belt that she'd been about to fasten. 'You shouldn't have stopped for me, Dr Tregarron. The bus was on its way.'

He shrugged. 'My good deed for the day.'

'*You* were never a Boy Scout!' she exclaimed in mock astonishment.

A smile tugged at his sensual lips. 'I doubt if you'd believe that I was ever a boy,' he said dryly.

Saffron unbuttoned the thin raincoat, disdaining to reply but suddenly struck by a mental image of a small boy with an unruly mop of dark curls, a gleam of mischief in his dark eyes and a reputation as the terror of Pethnavick. No doubt he'd bullied all the other little boys and kissed all the little girls whether they liked it or not, she thought, refusing to be softened by a foolish sentiment.

Jarvis glanced at her as she drew the scarf from her hair and shook out the gleaming tresses. She looked back at him with an almost defiant sparkle in her grey eyes and he smiled, warm and disarming.

'Shopping trip, Miss Pierce?'

His tone was pleasant if formal. Saffron was instantly on her guard. 'Yes. I've arranged to meet Sister James in the market square.'

He nodded. 'She's a nice girl. You seem to have made several friends in a short time.'

Saffron suspected that he was hinting at Tom's interest and Philip's friendliness and Clay's pursuit more than Bronwen's apparent liking for her. 'Surprised?' she countered defensively.

'A little. You're so prickly that I wonder how anyone manages to get near enough to know you,' he said bluntly, turning off the main road to take the quieter and more scenic route to the town.

'I'm not prickly with people I like.'

'Well, that tells me exactly where I stand,' he said dryly.

'I didn't think you were in any doubt!'

'Isn't it time we called a truce, Saffron?'

She was startled by the unexpected warmth of the words, the easy intimacy in his use of her name. She sat stiffly by his side, staring at the winding ribbon of country road, refusing to soften because he already threatened to invade her heart and destroy her peace of mind. He was best kept at a safe distance.

'No one declared war.'

He laughed. 'My dear girl, you commenced hostilities almost at our first meeting and seem to be armed with fresh ammunition every time we meet!'

'While you wave the white flag?' she demanded scornfully.

'I'm doing my best,' he pointed out.

Saffron was silent. She admitted that he had made one or two overtures towards peaceful co-existence. A kiss in the moonlight. An invitation to board his boat. This lift in his car to Helston. All very surprising—and rather suspect, she decided firmly, remembering another Tregarron's unwelcome attentions. They were probably tarred with the same brush!

'I'm not suggesting total surrender,' he went on, as though he knew what was in her mind. 'But you could give a little ground without losing face, you know. You could have dinner with me tonight, for instance.'

It was very unexpected. Saffron looked at him, startled. 'I'm sorry. I can't.'

His hands tightened on the steering wheel. 'Can't—or won't?'

'I'm going to the rugger club dance with Bronwen and her friends.' Saffron wondered why she felt that he merited an explanation for the refusal. She wouldn't have agreed if she'd been free that evening. But she might have been very tempted, she admitted honestly.

'Scarcely your scene,' he told her bluntly.

She shrugged. He could be right, but she resented the arrogant assumption that he knew what would or wouldn't appeal to her idea of an enjoyable evening. 'I've promised to go.'

'And you don't break promises?'

'Not if I can help it.'

'Then promise to have dinner with me another night,' he said promptly.

Saffron shook her head, sternly compelling herself to resist the temptation in the smile that lurked in the dark eyes and hovered about the sensual mouth of this attractive man. 'I never make promises that I know I won't want to keep, Dr Tregarron,' she said sweetly.

His smile faded abruptly. 'You really are the most difficult, bloody-minded . . .' He broke off with a rueful laugh. 'I've never met a woman quite like you! What *do* you have against me, for heaven's sake?'

'Let me see . . . Rudeness. Arrogance.' Saffron began to count off the failings on her slender fingers, a sparkle in her eyes and a challenge in the tilt of her chin. 'Selfishness. Male chauvinism. Shall I go on? I can think of lots more!'

He brought the car to an abrupt halt on a lonely stretch of the country road. Saffron looked at him in wary surprise, wondering if he meant to abandon her in the middle of nowhere. He looked quite annoyed enough to do it.

He looked back at her, mouth tightening. Then he suddenly leaned to kiss her, quick and hard and determined. Saffron drew back, stiffening with shock and anger and the leaping excitement that the fleeting touch of his warm lips had sparked.

She glowered at him. 'I suppose that's the price a girl has to pay for a lift in your car!'

'Cornish currency,' he agreed mockingly. 'Fair exchange, surely?'

Seeing the glow of satisfaction in the dark eyes at the response that she hadn't been able to help or hide, Saffron didn't smile. 'I wish I'd waited for the bus!'

He smiled. 'You might not have fancied the bus conductor,' he warned.

'I don't fancy *you*!' she told him quickly and without truth.

He searched the proud and pretty face, the defiant grey eyes, for confirmation of the claim. Then he said grimly, 'I wish I didn't fancy you, Saffron. You're a complication that I didn't need!' He took her face firmly between his two hands and kissed her again, long and lingeringly.

Saffron was caught up in the vortex of passion that trembled throughout his powerful body. Resolve fled in an instant and she allowed her lips to part and quicken and warm to his ardour. He put an arm about her and drew her close, stifling the weak murmur of protest with his deepening kiss, and she felt his hand on her breast in a slow and sensuous caress that swirled her senses with a kind of intoxication . . .

CHAPTER NINE

HIS TOUCH sent shivers of delight rippling through her body, and the wave of wanting seemed ready to disregard every consideration but the need for emotional and physical fulfilment in this man's ardent embrace.

With a considerable effort of will, Saffron thrust him away. 'No! That's enough!' she said fiercely, dismayed by the flooding response to his kiss, his touch, his hard and urgent body against her own.

The heavy beat of his heart was echoed by the throb of the pulse in the powerful column of his throat. 'This isn't the time or the place,' he agreed, a little unsteadily, straightening in his seat. 'But I *will* have you, Saffron . . .'

A heady mix of anticipation and apprehension sent desire shafting down her spine and tingling in every vein.

'I don't think so,' she retorted, trying to sound firm, trying to sound outraged by the unmistakable meaning of the confident words.

'What has thinking to do with it? It's the way we feel that really matters,' he said softly. He laid his hand along her cheek in a caress that held the promise of further enchantment. 'You're lovely and I want you very much. I believe you want me.'

'Then you're mistaken, Dr Tregarron!'

It was a quick, almost angry protest prompted by a surge of pride. For wasn't he deeply in love with Delia? Didn't he mean to marry Delia at the earliest possible moment? She was just a passing fancy for a sensual man, she told herself sensibly. Like his cousin Clay, he only wanted her in a way that owed nothing to loving—or even liking. And he was infuriatingly sure of her response to that potent physical magnetism, damn his arrogance!

He sighed. 'Will you stop fighting me? All that passion and energy could be put to better use, you know,' he said gently. He smiled at her suddenly, warmly. 'Kiss me, Saffron. Kiss and be friends.'

For once, he wasn't commanding, imperious. The warmth that turned her name into an endearment and the quiet persuasion in that deep and melting voice shook her resolution and her foolish heart.

Saffron knew it was madness. She knew she would regret it, for he wasn't really interested in her friendship. Yet, scarcely knowing why she should wish to please or gratify him, she leaned to touch her lips to the smiling, sensual mouth, her heart pounding.

Jarvis caught her to him with a sudden, fierce urgency that startled her back to sanity. Instantly, she put both hands to that powerful chest to keep him at bay and her lips turned cool and unwilling as he kissed her. For just a moment longer he held her, and she sensed the tremor that ran through his frame and knew that he was only just in control of the tumultuous tide of desire.

Releasing her, he reached to grip the steering wheel with tense hands, breathing hard, a nerve jumping in his jaw.

'I suppose that's your idea of a *friendly* kiss,' she said coldly.

Jarvis looked at her with a smile glinting in his dark eyes. 'Disappointed? Next time I'll make it friendlier and I'll choose a different time and place. Next time watch out for fireworks!'

It was an apt warning, she thought ruefully. For with his arms about her and his lips on her own and that flame of passion leaping between them, she'd felt as if she was a spinning catherine wheel on the verge of exploding in a shower of sparks!

'There won't be a next time,' she said sharply. 'I'll make sure of that.'

He laughed softly. 'Not very convincing.' He turned the ignition key and the engine leaped into life. 'Try again.'

Saffron glowered. He didn't have an ounce of consideration for her pride! 'That's just what I'd expect from you! You can't believe that any woman would turn you down, I suppose? Well, this woman just did. I'm not interested, Dr Tregarron.'

'I don't know why you're so afraid of getting involved. You just don't trust me at all . . .' There was a hint of impatience behind the words.

'I may not trust you but I'm certainly not afraid! Not of you—or any man! I can take care of myself.'

'You may be doing so for the rest of your life if you aren't careful, Little Miss Independence,' he said mockingly as the car moved off in the direction of Helston. 'That's no way to get a husband.'

'What makes you think I'm looking for a husband?' she demanded indignantly.

He smiled. 'Didn't you say so the other day?'

Saffron suddenly recalled her words to Bronwen. So he *had* heard—and remembered. 'That was just a joke,' she said dismissively.

His smile deepened and she knew that he was merely being provocative—and she'd risen to the bait just as he'd anticipated.

'I thought you were setting your cap at van Wyk.'

'Well, I'm not! Nor Philip. Nor your cousin Clay,' she said coldly, forestalling further charges, sure that friendly interest as well as amorous attention had been exaggerated. In any place where men and women worked together, there was bound to be gossip. She didn't want Jarvis Tregarron to think that she was a flirt who might easily be persuaded to be wanton, too!

'Philip is too light-weight for you and Clay has a wife, even if he sometimes chooses to forget it. But Tom van Wyk is probably just the type to appeal to an ambitious nurse on the look-out for a suitable husband. Delia tells me that you're spending the day with him tomorrow.'

It was so carelessly said that she couldn't tell if he objected or not. There was really no reason why he should, she reminded herself firmly. 'Yes, sight-seeing.'

'It will be a good thing for you to get away from Pethnavick and your patient for a few hours,' he approved. 'You seem to find it hard to be objective about Delia and her problems.'

Saffron glanced at him with swift suspicion. 'Does that mean that you feel it will be better for Delia if I'm not around? I know you think I have too much influence over her!'

'Delia is easily influenced by too many people, I'm afraid,' he said smoothly. 'She has little mind of her own and wishes to please anyone who shows the least affection for her.'

'Then she must be wax in *your* hands!' Saffron was angered by the coolly critical censure. It seemed that even his love for Delia couldn't soften his ingrained intolerance and arrogance! Jarvis Tregarron just couldn't help being critical and contemptuous of people who didn't match up to his high standards. She wondered dryly if anyone could. He seemed to expect far too much from ordinary human beings!

'Not entirely. Like most weak people, she has a stubborn streak and will suddenly make up her mind to do something and stick to it at all costs. Usually something totally unwise or unsuitable. Like marrying Ivor, for instance. That marriage would have been a disaster if fate hadn't stepped in to put an end to it.'

Saffron hated that cool, unemotional statement without being able to analyse just *why*, except that Jarvis ought to feel the loss of his brother and he ought to feel for Delia's unhappiness more deeply than he apparently did. She didn't want to believe that he was hard and harsh enough to regard it as a judgment on a foolish girl who'd had the temerity to jilt him, and a punishment for the brother who'd aided and abetted her. Even *he* couldn't be that arrogant—or that paranoid! But it sounded that way and it lowered him in her estimation— and she didn't want to think badly of him.

'You seem to be shocked into silence,' he said dryly after a moment or two of waiting for her to voice the feelings that obviously burned in her spirited breast.

Saffron said in low tones, 'That was a dreadful thing to say.'

He shrugged. 'Truth is seldom pretty. The truth is that Delia will go on loving Ivor for much longer than she might have done if he'd lived to disappoint her and spoil her romantic dream of happy ever after.'

'You're a cynic.'

'I'm a realist,' he amended.

'Why are you so sure that they wouldn't have been happy?'

She was curious, for everyone else spoke of the couple's obvious love for each other, their glowing happiness, Delia's radiance as a bride and Ivor Tregarron's evident pride in the lovely girl he was marrying. Surely they'd had as much chance as any other bride and groom of real and lasting happiness? Even if they had reached out to take it at Jarvis Tregarron's expense?

'Love can be a dangerous weakness,' he said brusquely, like a man who knew and had struggled with the self-same threat to his pride and resolution. 'Ivor would have denied her nothing because he loved her too much, and Delia would soon have despised a husband she couldn't respect. A weak woman needs a strong man.'

'Someone like yourself?' It was rather too quick. But Saffron was smarting from fierce resentment of a love that had survived long after he should have salvaged both heart and pride from the debris of a broken engagement. It seemed that Jarvis was just as weak as everyone else when it came to loving . . .

'Yes,' he agreed coolly. 'Delia would have realised that within a very short time.'

He was insufferable, Saffron thought crossly. Much too sure of himself! But, deep down, she admired the frank and fearless honesty, the obvious contempt for hypocrisy and pretence. A woman would always know where she was with him, she decided impulsively. He said what he meant—and he seemed to mean exactly what he said.

'It can't have been easy for you to wish them happiness,' she said carefully.

He was suddenly angry. 'Well, I did, damn you! Do you think I wanted her hurt, unhappy? Do you think it would have given me satisfaction to see them both miserable? Is that how you see me, for God's sake?'

'It might have been a very natural reaction. Very human . . .'

'Human, maybe! But not very worthy. Ivor and I were very close. Delia drove a wedge between us and I felt it deeply. But I didn't grudge them their happiness. I was angry with the pair of them, but I tried not to let it show too much. I'm accused of too much pride, but it kept me from saying and doing a number of things that I would now be regretting very much. I'm thankful for that!'

Saffron's heart wrenched with compassion—and something more that was dangerously akin to love. Afraid of betraying that surge of emotion, she said nothing.

'As a stranger, you can't be expected to know that it's alien to my nature to delight in the misery of people I care about,' he swept on coldly as she made no response to such an unusual relaxation of his reserve.

'Oh, I'm sure it is,' she said quietly, hurt by the tone that seemed to put her firmly outside the bounds of his caring and concern. She was unaware that her tone lacked conviction.

His mouth tightened. 'You're sure it *isn't*,' he countered dryly. 'However, we shall never know if that marriage would have been a success. Now there's a danger that Delia will idealise Ivor's memory to the extent that no other man can take his place. But that won't prevent her from marrying again—and soon.'

It was said so confidently that Saffron was sure that he couldn't have declared his love or his intentions more plainly. She'd known all along that he intended to marry Delia as soon as convention and her health allowed, of course. So there was no rhyme or reason to the absurd sinking of her heart.

Hurt welled and spilled over into words. 'You'll see to that, I expect!' she said tartly.

Jarvis raised a surprised eyebrow. 'I shall certainly encourage her to consider it,' he agreed smoothly.

'*Encourage her!* You mean that you'll bully her into re-marrying,' she said bitterly. 'The poor girl doesn't stand a chance against a juggernaut like you! You just won't allow her to run her own life, will you?'

'When I attempt to run *your* life, you will have the right to protest, Miss Pierce,' he told her icily, the dark flush of anger staining his handsome face. 'I think I know rather better than you do what is best for Delia.'

His foot pressed down hard on the accelerator pedal until the car was moving at almost reckless speed along the narrow approach road to the town. Saffron looked away from him, studying the houses that were beginning to crowd upon each other on both sides of the road with unseeing eyes.

Soon he would drop her in the market square and drive away, still angry, still resenting what he obviously felt to be unwarranted interference. There was a hard little lump in her throat that she didn't choose to analyse as hurt. She didn't want to believe that he could hurt her quite so much with that fierce determination to marry Delia at all costs.

They were no nearer to being friends than they'd ever been, she thought heavily. She didn't do herself a scrap of good by constantly quarrelling with him. But, remembering those heady kisses and the fierce flame of a mutual passion, she knew that they could easily become lovers. Was that what she wanted, with his marriage to Delia looming in the uncomfortably near future? He would take all that she was fool enough to give and then walk out of her life. Did she really want him so much that she would risk everything for a brief enchantment in his arms?

Saffron's heart lurched in sudden alarm as they seemed to avoid collision with an oncoming van by a last-minute miracle rather than his skill as a motorist. 'Hey! Slow down!' she exclaimed sharply. 'Do you want me dead, too?'

The impulsive, ill-considered words were spoken before she could check them and it was only later that she realised their full enormity. His immediate reaction merely told her that he fiercely resented her thoughtless remark.

For he brought the car to a sudden halt and then leaned to open the passenger door in peremptory manner. The accidental brush of his arm across her breasts set Saffron tingling all over again but the grim set to his mouth and the expression in his eyes chilled her heart.

'Is this Market Street?' she asked carefully, sensing the tension that told her that he was only just holding on to his temper.

'This is the parting of the ways, Miss Pierce,' he said deliberately and with a meaning it was impossible to mistake. 'You can walk the rest of the way to Market Street in a few minutes. First right, second left.'

Saffron hesitated, although he wasn't giving her a choice. 'I'm sorry if I offended you, Jarvis,' she said quietly. 'It was just words. I didn't mean anything.'

'That runaway tongue will get you into serious trouble one day, I suspect.' His tone was scathing and very cold. His eyes were chips of black ice.

'I'm afraid I hurt you,' she persisted.

'Forget it.'

She didn't think that *he* would. She looked at the hard, handsome face that had closed against her with such finality and her heart plummeted.

She scrambled from the car, murmuring awkward thanks that he didn't bother to acknowledge, and then turned to walk in the direction that he'd indicated. The Jaguar shot past her at speed and she looked after it, biting her lip, a dreadful churning in the pit of her stomach and pain radiating from the heavy lump that was her heart.

Bronwen was waiting in the little café with the green-striped awning, as they'd arranged, and she smiled with evident relief as Saffron appeared at the door.

'There's late that old bus can be!' she exclaimed. 'I thought you must have missed it.'

Saffron looked slightly uncomfortable as she slipped into a chair. 'I didn't come in by the bus, after all. Dr Tregarron gave me a lift in his car.' She turned to the waitress in the green-striped overall. 'Oh, tea, please— and some of those delicious pastries,' she ordered, glad of the interruption.

Bronwen wasn't so easily diverted. As soon as the woman moved out of earshot, she smiled at Saffron. 'Dr Tregarron, is it? Which one, now, I wonder? Spoiled for choice I am, see.' Her tone was suspiciously airy. 'Dr Fern, perhaps? Or Dr Clay with the Rover car and the rover hands to match?'

'Jarvis,' Saffron said shortly, putting an abrupt end to the light-hearted speculation, discovering that she suddenly lacked a sense of humour where the Tregarrons were concerned. There were too many of them—and one in particular seemed to have become much too important in a very short space of time.

'Dr Jarvis. There's surprise, then!' Bronwen's mischievous tone and dancing brown eyes implied the opposite. 'And argued all the way here, is it?'

Saffron mustered a smile. 'Does it show?' She hoped the Welsh girl wasn't perceptive enough to guess that they hadn't spend the entire time since leaving Pathnavick in argument! Very strangely, most uncomfortably, she felt as if the doctor's ardent kisses had left their mark on her for all the world to see, despite their lack of real meaning.

'No, no. But you never seem to meet without the sparks flying.'

In more ways than one, Saffron thought wryly. 'We do

seem to rub each other the wrong way,' she agreed lightly. 'Detestable man! How do you manage to get on so well with him, Bronwen?'

'Oh, I just do my job and try not to tell him how to treat his patients,' Bronwen said slyly.

Saffron looked at her quickly—and instantly acquitted her of malice. She wasn't that kind of girl.

'Listening at doors then, is it?' she said, smiling, teasing her friend's idiomatic Welshness.

'Not guilty!' Bronwen protested promptly. 'But you *were* overheard by someone who couldn't resist remarking on your courage in standing up to our Jarvis. He doesn't usually take at all kindly to being challenged by a nurse—or anyone else!'

'What makes you suppose that he swallowed any of the things I said to him? You may have noticed that we aren't on the best of terms,' Saffron said with feeling.

'You're still with us!'

'That's only a matter of time, believe me! I'm only at the clinic on sufferance as far as he's concerned.' The knowledge that the words were only too true weighed heavily on her spirits although she spoke with admirable lightness. She wasn't used to being so thoroughly disliked—or used to being pursued by men with only one thought in mind, who turned nasty when they met with rebuff!

The rain had stopped by the time they left the café to mingle with the shopping crowds. Saffron wasn't consciously looking for Jarvis Tregarron but her heart gave an odd little leap every time she saw a dark head towering above others on the swarming pavement, or caught a glimpse of a tall man in a similar grey suit.

He hadn't told her what brought him into Helston that morning. For all she knew, he'd been on his way to another town and was miles away by that time. Out of sight ought to be out of mind, she knew, and did her best to think of something other than his too-attractive face and the disturbing glow in his dark eyes that had so suddenly turned to indifference.

Usually, she liked to shop. But she couldn't seem to bring her mind to it that morning. She bought the wrong shade of lipstick, dithered between two blouses and finally plumped for the one that she knew she'd loathe when she was in her right mind. When Bronwen wanted her opinion of a dress in a shop window she answered absently and generally behaved in idiot fashion—and all because of a kiss or two from a man that she had never meant to like!

Lunch was a drink and a snack in a crowded pub with Bronwen's boyfriend and two of his rugger team-mates. Saffron told herself that she was enjoying the light banter and blatant admiration of two husky Cornishmen. Then she caught sight of Jarvis standing at the bar with an attractive and very elegant woman and knew that she wasn't enjoying herself at all.

She'd known that there had to be women in his life apart from Delia, of course. He was too sensual to be celibate and he was undeniably attractive to women, with his impressive height and build, distinctive good looks and eligible status as doctor and Tregarron. Seeing his smile, seeing the warmth in those deep-set dark eyes, Saffron's heart turned over in her breast, even though the smile and the glow was for another woman.

He was the best-looking man in the place. A real man in every sense of the word, Saffron decided, suddenly impatient with the burly buffoons on either side of her. They probably thought that drinking beer and singing bawdy songs and hurling themselves about a rugger pitch to the roar of the crowd was proof of their masculinity. She wanted more than that in a man and Jarvis had a lot of qualities that she admired and respected, she admitted.

She was too honest to beat about the bush or to deceive herself any longer. She looked across the crowded bar at Jarvis Tregarron and knew that the way she felt about him was suspiciously like loving. Real and lasting—and painful!

Was that why she'd been so willing to give up a good job at the Howlett Memorial and take a chance on liking the work and the people at the Tregarron Clinic? Was that why she'd tried so hard to dislike the man who'd only offered her a job because it would please the woman he loved and meant to marry? And was that why she'd thought of little else but a dark-haired doctor and his impact on her heart and mind ever since she'd arrived in Pethnavick?

If so, then she was a fool . . .

CHAPTER TEN

As THOUGH he sensed her gaze, but probably only irritated by the noisy banter and laughter of her small party, Jarvis turned and looked directly at Saffron. She felt slightly embarrassed. She wanted to rush over to him and assure him that they weren't her choice of friends or her kind of people and that she wasn't comfortable in their company. Then she wondered why she should assume that he cared how or with whom she spent her free time. For he looked at her without disapproval or mockery. Or the slightest degree of interest, she realised abruptly.

His glance swept over her with complete indifference and then he turned back to the woman at his side. Not even the glimmer of a smile or the hint of a nod for her or Bronwen, she thought angrily, smarting at the unmistakable snub. *Dr Arrogant MD!*

It was not only her pride that suffered. Her heart ached for the shattering of a foolish dream that she'd scarcely known that she cherished. Was that how it would always be in the future—had he lost all interest in her? Did he find it so hard to forgive a few thoughtless words? Had she been given a glimpse of a kind of heaven only to have the door slammed sharply in her face?

Leaving the pub with Bronwen some minutes later, the men staying behind for another pint, Saffron nodded in the direction of the couple who had moved to a corner table and were deep in conversation, apparently oblivious to everything but each other.

'That's a good-looking girl with our boss,' she said as lightly and incuriously as she could.

With a glance at the couple, Bronwen followed her out to the street. 'Audrey Carslake. Good-looking *and* clever,' she obliged. 'She's a solicitor and the daughter of a local magistrate. Lots of money and all the right connections. Just right for our Jarvis.'

'I suppose they've known each other for ever.' It was carefully casual. So was her expression as Saffron paused to look at a selection of shoes in a shop window. 'I need some new sandals . . .'

'They met last year when she brought her appendix to the clinic and left without it. I think she was interested then but he wasn't playing. Patient, see—and he was involved elsewhere. But they've been seeing a lot of each other lately, I'm told. I like this season's lower heel, don't you? More comfortable.'

Bronwen was just as casual, tone and manner accepting a newcomer's interest in her employer as perfectly natural. If she cherished a growing suspicion that Saffron's interest was rather more than ordinary, it didn't show. For a few moments they discussed the merits of the various styles of shoe on show, Saffron longing to know more about the relationship between doctor and solicitor and unable to ask.

'I don't think he's so interested,' Bronwen went on as they walked further down the narrow and bustling street. 'I think he just took up with her when the rumours started circulating. To give the old gossips something else to talk about, see.'

'Rumours?' Saffron felt trepidation catch at her heart. Just as if she sensed what was coming and knew that she wasn't going to like it!

Bronwen hesitated, shrugged. 'There's silly people can be with their tongues making bad worse, isn't it?

You know he was engaged to Delia and what she did?'

Saffron nodded, wondering if there was anyone in this part of the world who *didn't* know, wondering how Jarvis had endured the public sympathy and speculation—and possibly even a sneaking satisfaction in some quarters that the famous Tregarron pride had been trampled in the dust.

'Ivor, too. His own brother. There's hard for a man to live with, isn't it?' Bronwen shook her head, brown eyes warm with compassion. 'Bad enough, and worse to come with that terrible accident—and then a lot of nasty talk that he wanted Ivor dead and made it happen. Nasty, indeed! Sick I was, when I heard what people were saying.'

Saffron felt sick, too. She recalled the hasty words that she'd hurled at him. *Do you want me dead, too?* He must have believed them calculated to hurt. He must have felt that she knew and believed what the gossips had circulated about his brother's death.

'How could he be responsible, for heaven's sake!' she protested hotly. 'It was an accident, and it happened miles from here!'

'The police found that Ivor's car had faulty steering, a loose pinion or something like that. Jarvis knows a lot about cars. Spends hours working on them. His hobby, it is.' Bronwen's tone was carefully non-committal.

'People think he tampered with the car, is that what you're saying? How horrible!' Shocked, Saffron stopped short in the middle of the narrow pavement.

She might not have known Jarvis long or well, but she knew he was incapable of anything so wicked and she was ready to defend him to the death against such cruel and malicious slander. He was a doctor, dedicated to saving and preserving life. He was no cold-blooded murderer who'd wreaked a terrible revenge on a brother who'd injured him! It was a monstrous suggestion!

'Do they say that he wanted to kill Delia, too?' she demanded with fierce contempt. 'People are such fools.'

An elderly woman shopper grumbled at them for blocking the footpath. Bronwen took Saffron by the arm and urged her along, murmuring an apology.

'A jealous man will do anything,' she said wryly.

Saffron looked at her, indignant. 'But it's absurd! He couldn't do such a thing!'

Bronwen shrugged. 'Oh, I agree with you. But he isn't a popular man. Too proud, see. He doesn't go out of his way to be liked and he speaks his mind too bluntly. So he's made a few enemies who say that he doesn't mourn Ivor as he should. Tregarrons hide their feelings well. They also say that he means to marry Delia as soon as he can. Well, that's obvious . . .'

'Yes.' Saffron was suddenly uncomfortable, remembering that she had doubted, too. Had thought him harsh, unfeeling, and only waiting for the dust to settle before he took steps to marry his brother's lovely widow. Perhaps the last was true. She would never believe the rest!

In common with everyone else, Bronwen believed that he was still in love with Delia, she thought heavily. *She* had never doubted it. So it was all the more foolish that she'd allowed herself to fall in love with him.

It was unfortunate that head and heart were so troubled by a newly-admitted love that she couldn't enjoy the dance that evening or the day she spent with Tom van Wyk.

She did her best to appreciate the company and the conversation of the man who tried so hard to give her a lovely day. He arrived punctually at eleven and Saffron went out to meet him in a cool white cotton skirt and sun top. The day promised to be very hot. With her hair curling loosely on her shoulders and framing her face, and a bright smile for him pinned firmly to her lips, she looked very pretty and Tom's expression brightened visibly.

She was almost sorry that Jarvis wasn't around at the time to see the way that Tom took both her hands in his own and smiled down at her with a flattering warmth in his blue eyes. He settled her in his car with a blend of courtesy and friendliness that was in marked contrast to the brusqueness of the other man, who was either extremely hostile or much too ardent, according to mood and moment. Jarvis was so unpredictable. Tom van Wyk was too predictable, she decided. He was attractive and personable but it was a little too late for her to be impressed or attracted. Yet he was exactly the kind of man that she'd always hoped to meet, she reminded herself. Distinguished, successful, uncomplicated. The ideal husband for a nurse like herself!

They stopped for a drink in a little fishing village that was quaint and picturesque with its tiny harbour and huddle of stone cottages. They sat on the low wall and admired the view of St Michael's Mount, watched the fishermen mending their nets and listened to the plaintive cry of the seagulls and the steady slap of the sea against the stones.

They reached Penzance in time for lunch and a brief stroll around the town before driving on to Land's End, the bleak promontory on the Atlantic. For all the awesome and majestic beauty of the famous spot, Saffron felt it to be unfriendly and she wasn't sorry to leave it behind. They returned by a different route, stopping at Mousehole for the cream tea that was just as delicious as he'd promised.

'It's been a lovely day, Tom,' she said warmly. It wasn't his fault that she'd been in no mood to enjoy it or that she'd constantly hankered for a different companion.

'It isn't over yet. It's a long drive back to Pethnavick and my car might run out of petrol,' he warned mischievously. 'We might be stranded miles from anywhere and be forced to shelter for the night at a lonely inn where the only accommodation is a double room with a vast four-poster bed.'

'Which you'd insist on giving up to me while you made yourself comfortable on the floor!'

'Of course,' he agreed, but the look in his eyes warned her that he was a man like any other—he would promise anything but would still be quick to take advantage of an opportunity to make love to a pretty girl.

'That kind of thing only happens in romantic novels,' she said lightly. 'I shouldn't think it *could* be romantic in real life—and is it possible to be stranded in these days of telephones and a string of garages right across the country?'

Tom heaved a mock sigh. 'Trust a nurse to be practical! If the car broke down instead of running out of petrol I suppose you could put it to rights. There's no hope for us poor men with today's girls. Romance is out of fashion and there's no such thing as a damsel in distress any more.'

Saffron smiled at him. 'Never mind,' she comforted. 'Men have a lot more respect for a woman's abilities these days, and if your car did break down you'd probably be very grateful if I did put it to rights.'

The consultant studied her, amused. 'And could you?'

'I'd have a try. I know something about cars, thanks to a former boyfriend who was always tinkering with them and liked to have me lend a hand. It's rather like learning theatre procedures, you know. One can learn a lot just by listening and observing and passing instruments!'

'Admirable! Does Jarvis know about that useful accomplishment? Cars are his hobby. Once he learns that he has a fellow-enthusiast on his staff he'll never want to let you go!'

Saffron's heart gave an absurd leap in response to the unexpected mention of a certain doctor's name and she thought wistfully that she'd prefer to be wanted for a much better reason than her aptitude as a car mechanic!

'I'm not exactly an enthusiast. You could say that I was young enough and green enough at the time not to mind taking second place to a car. But I soon grew out of that. I don't mind fair and reasonable competition but a girl likes to feel that she occasionally comes first in a man's life!' she declared brightly.

Tom smiled. 'I suspect that your boyfriend was also young and green. You'd certainly come before anything else in the life of a mature man!'

'Provided he isn't keen on cars or rugger—and isn't a dedicated doctor. I've known some mature men who were a combination of all three!'

It was light-hearted banter and Saffron was glad that there was no degree of unwelcome sentiment in his tone or manner. She felt they were already friends but would never be more. They both sensed that the vital spark of romance was missing from the relationship. They liked each other and enjoyed each other's company, but that was all.

Saffron knew without a shadow of doubt that he wasn't the kind of man that she'd been destined to love. Heart and mind and body all hungered for a very different man with a passionate intensity. Her heart swelled with longing for Jarvis Tregarron and the thought of him constantly crept into her mind. Her body had come swiftly and gloriously to life in his ardent embrace.

Her usually level head hadn't stood a chance against her unexpectedly wilful heart, she thought wryly. It was much too late for caution or common sense, or for considering the dangers of falling headlong in love with a man who would never want her as she wanted him . . .

Saffron didn't sleep very well that night, despite a surfeit of sun and fresh air and the excellent dinner that had rounded off a pleasant day with the consultant. Anxiety seemed to be nagging at her mind and heart throughout the long night.

She had been away from Pethnavick for several hours and Jarvis had been free to spend the entire day with Delia if he'd wished. It seemed much too soon, but it was still possible that he had talked Delia into marrying him in the near future, she felt. Hadn't he told her to forget the clinic and her patient in such a way that she'd challenged him with resenting her influence over Delia? Deprived of that influence and a support that she seemed to need, had Delia weakly given in to a dominant man's persuasions that almost amounted to command?

Saffron's heart faltered at the mere thought of him married to Delia and lost to her forever. Then she reminded herself that there had never been any hope for any other woman who loved him. His unchanged and undying love for Delia put an end to all the foolish and futile dreaming.

It was almost dawn before she eventually fell into a restless and dream-filled sleep. As a result, she woke late and scrambled into her lilac uniform frock and hastily thrust her shining hair into a semblance of a knot on the nape of her neck. She skipped breakfast and the usual early morning gossip with her fellow-nurses and almost ran the short distance between the dower house and the clinic.

Bronwen was in her office when Saffron put her head round the door to announce her arrival in suitably apologetic tones.

'There's late you are, girl,' she said without reproach, glancing up from the papers on the desk, hand stilled in the act of filling in a form. 'And no one knowing if you were lost in some lonely spot between here and Land's End—or worse, indeed!'

Saffron laughed. She'd already discovered that the Welsh girl had a taste for the dramatic. 'No, I'm fine, and safely back in one piece.'

'Enjoy your day?' Bronwen's smile was warm but the brown eyes were rather wistful.

'Very nice.' Saffron hesitated, wondering. She had seen that look in her friend's eyes before, whenever Tom van Wyk was about or mentioned. She seemed content with Gary but was she secretly hankering for another man? Well, she was welcome to Tom, Saffron thought swiftly, and if she could do anything to further the cause she wouldn't hesitate!

'He's a lovely man,' she went on lightly, using Bronwen's own turn of phrase for someone she liked and admired. 'Much more your type than mine, actually.'

'My type?' Bronwen shook her head, smiling. 'It isn't *me* that he fancies, girl.'

'Well, he talked enough about you,' Saffron told her firmly, suddenly realising that he *had* brought Bronwen's name into the conversation on several occasions. Perhaps he liked the warm-hearted ward sister but thought her too busy with another man to give him the encouragement he needed. Suspecting that she was rapidly tiring of the rugger-playing Cornishman who often put his sport and his mates before his girlfriend, Saffron hoped that Bronwen might be more encouraging in her attitude to the consultant if she could be persuaded to believe that he wasn't entirely immune to her charms.

But there was no time to discuss Tom van Wyk and his niceness that morning. Delia would be waiting, having resisted the efforts of any other nurse to get her out of bed and dressed for yet another session of the intensive course of physiotherapy. She had a streak of obstinacy in that sweet and gentle nature, and she insisted that Saffron should be the nurse to attend to her needs when she was on duty.

Leaving the office, Saffron saw Jarvis at the end of the corridor, talking to a nurse. It was silly to slow her steps when he was probably too intent on the conversation even to notice her, she told herself sternly. But she did hesitate, nevertheless.

Dark head bent courteously to listen, hands thrust into the pockets of the white coat he wore over his dark suit, he looked every inch the clever and competent physician—and so attractive that her heart tilted painfully.

Loving *hurt*, she'd discovered. And it hurt all the more because there was no chance of happiness with him. He'd whisked her heart out of her keeping before she knew it and without even trying. But she meant as little to him as the attractive Audrey Carslake, with whom he'd spent some time that weekend.

Probably less, Saffron amended bleakly, as she recalled the way he'd looked and smiled and laughed with the solicitor. *She* was a friend. Saffron had merely been a fleeting fancy which hadn't survived yet another clash of temperaments.

With a cool smile pinned to her lips, she walked

briskly towards the doctor and nurse, but the latter abruptly vanished into a patient's room with a whisk of starched skirts so that Jarvis was the only recipient of that proud and rather defiant smile, after all. It faded as his eyes narrowed in the way that she'd come to recognise as the prelude to an attack. She braced herself for some sardonic comment.

'You were late, Nurse Pierce,' he said, without preliminary. 'May I know why?'

'I've explained to Sister James. I overslept.' She didn't even try to infuse an apology into the words, resenting the arrogance of his attitude.

'Where did you oversleep?' he demanded brusquely.

Surprise widened her eyes. '*Where?*' she echoed. 'I don't know what you mean.'

Annoyance snapped his brows together as though he suspected her of fencing with him. 'Did you sleep at the dower house last night? Or somewhere else? That's what I mean!'

Saffron was furious, realising that the obvious and insulting implication of the words could only be prompted by his knowledge that she'd spent the previous day with Tom van Wyk. He seemed to think that she might have spent the night with him, too!

'That's my business, don't you think?' she said angrily. 'I don't have to answer to you for where I spend my nights, Dr Tregarron!'

His mouth tightened into a grim line. 'I don't give a damn where you spend your nights. But Miss Currie was concerned about you, apparently. She knew that you'd gone out for the day. It seems that no one knew if or when you'd returned. She has an overworked sense of responsibility, even towards nurses who can take care of themselves,' he swept on dryly. 'I know it's an archaic system but it will relieve everyone's mind if you remember to sign in as well as out in future.'

'It certainly is archaic! We're treated like schoolgirls!' Saffron protested hotly.

She was all the more indignant because she *had* forgotten—and Dorothy was inclined to fuss when nurses forgot to sign the book. They were mostly good about remembering and good-natured about a rule that reminded them all of their early training days and vigilant Home Sisters. They joked about it, in fact, declaring that it was designed to keep them on the straight and narrow by an over-anxious warden. Saffron didn't really mind any more than the others did. But Jarvis seemed to have a gift for putting her on the defensive, she thought bitterly, wishing they could meet once without clashing.

'No one else objects. It's really a matter of courtesy and consideration,' he said coolly.

'No doubt you feel that I'm lacking in both!'

Jarvis raised an amused eyebrow. 'I'm certainly not impressed by your track record to date,' he agreed, sardonically. 'In fact, I'm beginning to feel that offering you a job was a mistake. You're too much of a rebel with too much to say for yourself.'

'Perhaps you'd like me to resign!' In the heat of anger, Saffron laid herself wide open to an acceptance of that hasty suggestion—and she held her breath in sudden, overwhelming anxiety.

'Oh, for goodness' sake, Saffron!' With an obvious effort, he checked the involuntary, exasperated outburst. He looked at her for a long moment, an enigmatic expression in his eyes. Then he said wryly, 'I'd like you to behave like a reasonable and responsible nurse instead of being forever ready to do battle with me like some misguided Joan of Arc!'

The rueful amusement in eyes and voice effectively deflated her indignation. His unexpected smile was so warm, so disarming, that her heart abruptly welled with love and longing—and regret that they could never meet without coming to verbal blows. She wished she could admit to him frankly that she wanted to make love not war!

'Perhaps I *should* leave,' she said impulsively. 'I seem to dent your dignity every time I open my mouth.' It was true and it was scarcely surprising that he couldn't like her and didn't approve of her, she thought bleakly.

It was meant to be a tentative olive-branch, a rueful admission of fault. Saffron realised from the sudden darkening of his eyes and the instant death of his smile that he interpreted it as defiant flippancy.

'To hell with my dignity, I'm not a public monument!' he exploded. 'Go, if that's what you want! But for your own sake, not mine. I don't give a damn what you do!'

As he strode down the corridor, stiff with anger, Saffron looked after him with tears springing to her eyes at the realisation that they were a million light years from any kind of understanding. He was harsh, unyielding and totally unable to forgive and forget. He was the last man in the world that she ought to love—and there was nothing she could do about it.

She ought to have too much pride to stay. But she knew she couldn't go, even though there was no hope of any happiness for her in Pethnavick.

She liked the place and the people and she didn't mean to let Jarvis or anyone else drive her away before she was ready to leave, she thought defiantly.

The nurse came out of her patient's room with a curious glance at her, obviously having overheard some, at least, of that heated exchange. Saffron smiled at her with an admirable pretence of cheerful indifference and hurried along the corridor to Delia's room . . .

CHAPTER ELEVEN

LATER in the week, Saffron was summoned by an urgent call to assist in theatre. She went willingly, pleased to have an opportunity to put her nursing skills to better use than merely looking after the convalescent Delia or dealing with the routine care of a few orthopaedic patients.

Busily organising the routine daily cleaning of the two well-equipped theatres, Meredith was brisk but not unfriendly.

'Sorry it's such short notice, but one of my nurses has gone down with flu. Would you scrub up and assist Philip this morning, Saffron? He's doing a pyelolithotomy. I seem to recall that you had some months of working in theatres at Kit's and I expect you know the procedure.'

'Yes—and I'd love to assist,' Saffron said promptly. 'But I may be a little rusty. I haven't been inside an operating theatre since last year.'

'You'll have time to read up on it, and you'll have plenty of help from Philip. The patient is in constant pain and the pyelograph shows a large stone in the pelvis of the kidney. Philip doesn't want to delay the operation while we try to get hold of an experienced agency nurse.'

'I'm sure I can cope.'

'If you'd prefer to start with something less complicated you can scrub for Clay in my place,' Meredith suggested kindly. 'He's doing a fairly routine hysterectomy and I don't suppose he'll mind, in the circumstances.'

'No. I'll assist Philip. Gynae is rather more specialised, isn't it? I was runner at several of John Trevor's ops when I was at Kit's,' Saffron said firmly, referring to a well-known urological surgeon. 'And I've scrubbed for general surgery lots of times. I'll be fine.'

Having heard that Clay was a demanding and very quick-tempered surgeon who didn't suffer fools gladly, a typical Tregarron, she didn't hesitate to turn down the well-meant suggestion.

She had another reason, too. Meredith couldn't be unaware of her husband's interest in a newcomer but she didn't seem to hold it against her and Saffron didn't want to give her any cause to suspect that Clay's amorous attentions were being well-received or encouraged.

Men like Clay Tregarron who couldn't take no for an answer and assumed that a girl was playing hard to get, even if she wasn't interested, were an occupational hazard for a nurse and Saffron found it easy to dismiss the admiring glances, soft-spoken comments and not too subtle suggestions. She didn't think he would be so irresponsible as to neglect his surgery for flirtation while he had a patient on the operating table. But she didn't mean to take any chances with the patient's well-being or Meredith's liking or her own reputation.

Saffron changed out of the lilac frock into a sleeveless cotton theatre dress, concealed her shining hair in a mob cap and exchanged black brogues for theatre slippers. Then she tied the tapes of her mask behind her head and went into the annexe to scrub up with meticulous care.

While she soaped and scrubbed and rinsed her hands and arms to the required degree of aseptic cleanliness, she anxiously cast her mind back to her theatre days at Kit's and hoped she would do well enough to be offered the chance of a permanent place on Meredith's theatre team when Delia no longer needed her. And then she

remembered with a little pang that Delia would probably be married to Jarvis by then and she might wish to
put as many miles as possible between herself and
heartache.

Reminding herself sternly that an operating theatre
was no place for a nurse's personal worries and
apprehensions, Saffron dried her hands and arms on a
sterile towel and put on sterile gown and gloves with the
assistance of a runner nurse. Then she went into the
scrubbed and spotless theatre and began to lay out
gleaming instruments and count and list swabs, careful
not to touch any unsterile surface. She was relieved to
find that the procedure came vividly back to mind with
very little prompting as she laid scalpels and forceps,
scissors and retractors, artery clips and the diathermy
sets in readiness for the surgeon.

Philip arrived to scrub up, accompanied by his assistant, and nodded to her through the glass screen
that divided theatre and annexe, his eyes warm with
approval above the green mask. Saffron nodded to him
in return, a smile in her own eyes, and then went on with
the business of laying out needles and their holders and
sutures in their sterile packs.

She hoped that she appeared cool and composed, but
her heart was beating rather fast when the surgeon and
his assistant finally came into the theatre, gloved and
gowned, and another nurse trundled the patient on a
trolley from the adjoining ante-room, accompanied by
the anaesthetist.

'I heard you were helping out,' Philip said in his
friendly way. 'Not nervous, are you?'

'A little,' Saffron admitted frankly.

'No need to be.' Philip ran an approving eye over the
completed preparations. 'You seem to know exactly
what you're doing. But I'll tell you what I need as we

proceed and I don't anticipate any problems. I think you know Mike, don't you? And Stuart?'

Saffron was reassured by the friendliness of assistant and anaesthetist as they tried to put her at ease, and she forgot to be nervous as she reached for the sterile drapes that would cover all of the patient except for the operating area. A last-minute check of the instruments, and then Philip moved to the table and waited, hands poised.

'Ready to go, Saffron?' he asked courteously.

She nodded. 'Yes, I think so.'

'Quite happy to proceed?'

Her eyes smiled at him over the mask. 'Yes.'

He held out a hand and she gave him the scalpel he needed to make the first incision, slapping it into his palm in the approved manner and saying what it was as she did so.

Within seconds the operation was under way, and Saffron was so busy admiring his technique and endeavouring to anticipate the instrument he would need fractionally before he put out a hand and named it that she had no time to doubt her ability to play her role to Philip's satisfaction. She simply got on with the job.

A good scrub nurse was an essential member of the surgical team in any theatre. She had to be alert and vigilant and thoroughly familiar with instruments and procedures. She also had to combine a cool head and confident work with a quietly relaxed manner, which minimised the tension of operating for long periods beneath hot arc lights.

Philip was a good surgeon, his skilful hands probing for the kidney stone, rapidly locating it and then easing it for access. Its prompt removal with sucker and forceps drew a little sigh of satisfaction from him.

'She should feel a lot better for being without that item of excess baggage,' he said lightly as he dropped the pea-sized kidney stone into a bowl of saline fluid. 'I'll just put a stitch into this kidney and then we'll be ready to begin closing her up, I think.'

Saffron handed him the prepared suture needle and then began to count swabs with careful precision, assisted by the runner nurse who stood by the counting stand where the used swabs were displayed.

It seemed almost too soon to Saffron before the last suture had been set in place, the last swab checked off on the list and the patient was ready to be wheeled away to the recovery room.

She realised just how much she'd enjoyed the morning's work, so very different to the routine nursing of an orthopaedic ward. She knew, without conceit, that she'd acquitted herself well, too.

Philip pulled off gown and gloves and dropped them into the 'dirty' bin. 'Well done, Saffron,' he applauded warmly. 'You were great! Wasn't she, Mike?'

The assistant surgeon nodded. 'Very smooth.'

Saffron's pleasure in the praise glowed in her grey eyes above her mask. 'I'm only grateful that I didn't disgrace myself!'

'Far from it! You were made for theatre work! So what on earth are you doing in orthopaedics?' Philip demanded.

She smiled. 'Gaining experience, I hope.'

'Well, if you ever want to take on a permanent job in theatre I'll welcome you with open arms, for one,' he told her firmly.

'I might hold you to that!'

'I mean it.' Philip glanced at the clock on the wall above the door. 'Well, that's it for today. It doesn't seem as if Elizabeth will be back for a few days so I hope you can stand in for her again tomorrow, Saffron.'

'I hope so, too.' It was non-committal because she

didn't know if Meredith would want to call on her services again and she didn't want to take it for granted.

As the two surgeons went away to the changing-room, Saffron felt suddenly deflated and tired and she realised that the morning had been a strain despite the pleasure she'd taken in the work. She'd been more tense than she'd known, more anxious to do well than she'd realised. She wondered if she'd been hoping that Jarvis would hear that she'd stepped so successfully into the breach and think better of the nurse whom he'd scornfully referred to as a rebel.

They'd scarcely spoken since that last heated exchange. Stiff with hurt and defiance of his dislike and disapproval, telling herself that if he wanted a responsible automaton who wouldn't challenge or provoke or disturb him that's exactly what she would be, Saffron had gone about her work at the clinic with quiet and dignified efficiency. She'd kept out of his way as much as she could and frozen him whenever her work or circumstances threw them together.

She knew that he was much too proud to attempt to thaw her with a word or a smile or a glance, even if he wanted to—and she doubted that he did. Not any more. He was so distant and forbidding and autocratic that she suspected he was deliberately underlining the gulf between a Tregarron and a mere nurse in his employ. She wished she could stop dreaming of bridging that gulf in some way some day, for they were such foolish dreams, doomed to disappointment . . .

Thrusting the thought of him from her mind, something that was becoming harder to do with every day that passed, Saffron turned her attention to the business of supervising the cleaning and tidying of the theatre, the removal of the dirty linen and taking used instruments for sterilisation.

Meredith was finally free to check on her protegée when Clay's hysterectomy patient was transferred from table to trolley and wheeled away to the recovery room. Minus gown and gloves but still wearing her mask, very slender in the thin theatre dress and a few damp tendrils of dark hair escaping from her cap, she pushed through the swing doors of the theatre where Saffron was busy with the last of the tidying-up.

Meredith smiled at her and looked about the gleaming theatre with obvious approval. Her own morning had been busy and demanding, owing to an unexpected complication in surgery, but she'd heard all about Saffron's excellent showing as a scrub nurse from a very complimentary Philip before he left the theatre suite. Now, seeing that Saffron had known what needed to be done and got on with doing it promptly and efficiently, Meredith knew that she had all the makings of a useful addition to her team.

'I've been hearing nice things about you,' she declared lightly. 'I gather you bore out all my claims for Kit's nurses!'

'Well, I hope I did. I think everyone was reasonably pleased with me, anyway.'

'*Very* pleased.'

'I thought I might have forgotten everything I ever know, but it seemed to come flooding back as soon as I began to scrub up. I always liked theatre work, of course. One is so involved.'

Meredith nodded. 'Most surgeons get so used to working with a particular scrub nurse that an unexpected change in the team can slow down an entire operation. I expect you saw that happen on occasions at Kit's?'

'Yes, sometimes.'

'I knew that Philip would see you through without a murmur of complaint, even if you weren't any good.

Clay would have lost his temper and thrown things, I'm afraid,' Meredith said frankly, with a rueful smile.

Saffron smiled. 'I knew surgeons like that at Kit's, too,' she said carefully, tactfully. As far as she was concerned, Clay Tregarron could throw anything but compliments in her direction and she wouldn't mind at all!

'In fact, Philip says that you're even better at assisting than Elizabeth,' Meredith went on. 'But that's strictly between you and me, of course. We don't want to hurt the poor girl's feelings and she's been here for years.'

'I wouldn't dream of pushing her out of a job, but I'd love to take her place until she comes back,' Saffron admitted candidly.

Meredith nodded, pleased. 'That's just what I hoped you would say. Maybe later on we can arrange for you to do theatre work on a regular basis—not necessarily scrubbing for Philip. Just now, I'm concerned with a temporary replacement for Elizabeth and I'd rather have you than an agency nurse. I've talked to Jarvis and he agrees that you'll be more useful to me than wasting your talents on routine nursing. So, if you're willing, I'd like you here for the next few days.'

'I'm very willing. But Delia may not be too pleased. She regards me as her personal nurse, you know,' Saffron reminded her.

'Oh, Jarvis can handle Delia.' Meredith was slightly impatient. 'He seems to feel that she'll make faster progress if she isn't quite so dependent on your physical and moral support, anyway.'

'Yes. He's said much the same thing to me,' Saffron agreed brightly, swallowing chagrin. No doubt he was delighted that she would be removed from his immediate orbit for a few days. She didn't believe that he was thinking solely of Delia's possible benefit from her absence.

'You can go off duty, now, Saffron. But bright and early in the morning, please. Eight o'clock start. Philip has a long list tomorrow and the first op is scheduled for nine-thirty.'

'What's on the list? I might need to spend the evening with a text book or two!'

'Oh, routine stuff. Philip does general surgery as well as our urological cases, you know. The first on the list is an appendicectomy and I think that's followed by a hernia, but I'll let you have full details later, if you like.'

Saffron showered and put on her lilac uniform frock to make her way down to the dower house. She loosened her slightly damp curls so that they fell about her shoulders—and then regretted the emphasis on her femininity, for she ran into Clay Tregarron as she was about to leave the theatre suite.

He was still in surgical greens but his mask dangled about his neck by its tapes. His dark eyes glowed at the sight of her as she walked along the corridor, and he paused, waiting for her to reach him.

Saffron glanced at him warily, hoping that he wasn't about to alienate Meredith and affect her own chances of theatre work with an indiscreet and totally unwelcome advance under his wife's nose.

'I heard you'd joined the team,' he said informally, smiling down at her warmly. 'Philip has been singing your praises.'

'That was nice of him.' Saffron prepared to walk on, dismissive. 'But I only did what I've been trained to do.'

'And did it very well, apparently. We can always use a good scrub nurse, and Meredith insists that Kit's produce the best in the world. She's biased, of course!'

'Kit's nurses stick together,' Saffron said meaning-fully. 'So I agree with her, naturally.'

'Oh, I'm not disputing the claim! I have every ad-miration for Kit's nurses,' he assured her, dark eyes dancing.

'You're biased, of course,' she reminded him smooth-ly, 'being married to one!' She walked on briskly, refus-ing to encourage him to linger in conversation with her in a corridor within sight and sound of the rest of the theatre staff. People were much too prone to put two and two together and make twenty-two of it, she thought dryly.

Descending the staircase that led down to the main hall of the old manor house, she saw Philip talking to Jarvis just outside the office. The surgeon glanced up and saw her and broke off his conversation to hurry to the foot of the stairs with the obvious intention of speaking to her before she left the building.

Conscious that Jarvis was watching with disapproving eyes, Saffron promptly quickened her steps to join the surgeon with every appearance of eagerness. She smiled at him with warmth and carefully didn't give the slightest indication that she was aware of the doctor's presence in the shadows.

'I've been waiting for you,' Philip greeted her. 'Come and have some lunch at the village pub, Saffron. You've earned a shandy and a sandwich at the very least, this morning.'

She laughed. 'Sounds tempting,' she declared lightly, deliberately throwing her voice so that Jarvis could hear from where he stood, watching and listening and making not the slightest move to come forward and add a word of approval to the flow of compliments she'd had from everyone else. No doubt he thought she was conceited enough!

'Be a devil and yield to temptation,' Philip urged, taking her by the arm and smiling down at her in friendly fashion.

'All right, I will,' she agreed impulsively. She was off duty for the rest of the day. Why shouldn't she spend a light-hearted hour with Philip, even if it was more than likely that he'd take advantage of an opportunity to talk at length about Delia with all the unconscious wistfulness of a man in love. It would show Jarvis that she wasn't dependent on his liking or friendship or approval, she thought with a surge of defiance to camouflage her hurt.

As they moved towards the door, laughing and talking, Jarvis looked after the couple for a tense moment. Then he went into his office and shut the door with a slam of irritation at this flirtatious nurse who seemed hell-bent on collecting Tregarron scalps. Saffron glanced over her shoulder in the direction of that sharp little sound and wished she could believe that it stemmed from his dislike and resentment of her camaraderie with everyone at the clinic but himself.

Philip looked back, too. 'No use expecting Jarvis to give you a word of praise,' he said carelessly, just as though he'd read her mind. 'He'd say you were just doing the job you were paid to do.'

'I don't expect it,' she said shortly. 'He'd probably choke if he had to pay me a compliment!'

Philip grinned. 'Case of Dr Fell, is it? You two certainly don't seem to like each other!'

Saffron shrugged. 'I don't lose any sleep over his lack of liking for me,' she said, without truth.

Philip waited discreetly in his car while she went into the dower house to change into off duty clothes. As a Tregarron, he was well-known. The distinctive lilac uniform would tell the world that she was a nurse from

the Tregarron Clinic. There was no need to set tongues
wagging.

Saffron found that lunch wasn't a matter of a shandy
and a sandwich at the local pub, after all. Philip had
reserved a table for two at a very expensive restaurant on
the outskirts of Helston. She thought it was typically
Tregarron behaviour that he'd made the reservation
before issuing the invitation, but what infuriated her so
much in Jarvis she seemed to find easy to overlook in his
endearing cousin.

They laughed and talked their way through an excellent and lengthy meal complete with the Muscadet that
she liked so much, and it was almost four o'clock when
they left the restaurant to return to Pethnavick.

Philip could scarcely be said to have drunk very much.
Saffron had consumed most of the wine in a rather
reckless attempt to wipe out the image of Jarvis Tregarron, which seemed to come too often between herself
and the good-looking face of the cousin who looked so
much like him, so it wasn't an excess of alcohol that
caused the accident.

Saffron only knew that at one moment they were
driving at normal speed along the coast road that wound
its way towards Pethnavick, and the next moment the
car was hurtling across the road towards a clump of
trees. She must have briefly lost consciousness. She
came round to the taste of blood in her mouth and found
an unconscious Philip slumped in the seat beside her,
grey-faced and breathing stertorously, blood pumping
from a deep gash in his leg. The bonnet and wing on his
side of the car had been crumpled like cardboard by the
impact with the tree.

Saffron realised that her first priority must be to stop
the bleeding—it looked as though an artery had been
ruptured. She scrambled from the car, bruised and

shaken and slightly dazed, wondering for a moment what to do. Then she ripped the hem from her cotton skirt and improvised a makeshift tourniquet, tying it round Philip's thigh just above the wound and tightening it until the blood ceased to pump his life away.

Then, with a shock, Saffron realised that his harsh and shallow breathing had stopped. There was no time to worry about the risk of moving him. Somehow, she managed to drag him from the car and position him on the ground. Then she began to force her own breath into his lungs, her mouth firmly over his, his nostrils pinched between her fingers. While she worked desperately to give him the kiss of life, she prayed that it wasn't too late and that she wouldn't faint before she could make his reluctant lungs work for themselves once more . . .

'All right, love, I'll take over now.'

Saffron had been concentrating so hard on her task that she hadn't registered the arrival of a car whose driver had witnessed the accident. He'd hurried to the nearest house to telephone for an ambulance and had then sped back to help if he could.

Saffron gave up her place reluctantly. But she soon realised that the man knew what he was doing and she knew she could relax. Within minutes, the ambulance arrived and they were both relieved of the responsibility that had been thrust upon them. Saffron found herself being helped across the road to the ambulance with an arm about her waist to keep her from sliding to the ground as her legs buckled beneath her. She'd risen to the emergency like a good nurse. But now she might be allowed to faint if she wished . . .

CHAPTER TWELVE

MORE shocked and shaken than hurt, apart from a nasty bump on her head and a cut mouth and some minor abrasions of arms and legs, Saffron was allowed to leave the hospital later that evening after examination and X-rays.

She was thankful, for she'd hated being on the receiving end of a thermometer and she was worried about Philip, who'd been taken directly to theatre. Now he was in Intensive Care with head and chest injuries as well as a broken and badly lacerated leg.

Saffron was flatly refused permission to see him, however. She wasn't a relative, and the fact that she was a nurse and had probably saved his life didn't cut any ice with the hatchet-faced sister in charge of the IC Unit.

Having been told that someone would come by car to collect her and take her back to Pethnavick, Saffron returned to wait in the Accident and Emergency Department, head aching, still shivery and wondering if the police had believed her insistence that Philip hadn't been drunk at the time of the accident.

It seemed a very long time before Jarvis stalked through the swing doors, the look on his handsome face boding ill for someone. Probably herself, she thought heavily. He was the last person she'd expected to concern himself about her and she rose uncertainly, colour coming and going in her small face.

'Looking for me?' she asked flippantly, to conceal the trembling of her heart, the sudden weakness of a longing to be held and comforted and reassured in his strong arms.

His scowling glance swept her from head to toe. He was taut with suppressed fury, Saffron realised, heart sinking. She had been through an unpleasant experience and it wasn't fair that he should glower as though she was entirely to blame, she thought, close to crying and proudly determined that he shouldn't reduce her to tears. Her chin went up.

'*You* seem to be all in one piece, anyway,' he said curtly.

'Cause for regret?' she challenged, smiling to hide her hurt. He didn't seem at all thankful that she'd escaped serious injury.

He looked as though he wanted to hit her. 'My only regret is that Philip was fool enough to take *you* any-where at any time,' he ground through clenched teeth. 'If you're ready, let's get out of here!' He seized her arm, turning towards the door, trembling with anger.

Saffron winced as his hard fingers found a bruise on her forearm. 'You're hurting,' she said quietly. But the pain of his grip was nothing compared to the pain that radiated from her heart and threatened to engulf her entire being.

He hustled her from the department and into the main hall of the hospital. 'I'd like to break your bloody neck!' he told her grimly.

People were staring, speculating, smiling. Saffron wrenched her arm free. 'Look, just go, will you!' she said tensely. 'I'll get a taxi. I'll get someone else to drive me back. I don't want to be with you. Just leave me alone, I've had enough for one day!' Her voice rose and shook on the last words.

Pausing, Jarvis looked down at her with scorn in the

dark eyes. 'About to have hysterics? Good. It will give me just the excuse I need!'

Not doubting what he meant, Saffron slapped *him*, hard, her hand leaping to the lean, mocking face almost of its own volition, compelled by hurt and shock and outraged pride. Then she sped to the outer doors of the hospital and whisked through them into the cool shadows of the evening, heart pounding and tears streaming. She walked blindly towards the gates through the stream of evening visitors, needing to escape, hating him—and achingly aware that he would certainly hate her for making him the talk of the county with that impulsive and angry blow.

Jarvis caught her before she'd gone many yards, swung her round. 'What the hell do you think you're doing?'

'Making my own way! I don't need you!' Saffron fought tears and faced him defiantly.

He gave her a little shake with strong hands on her shoulders. 'That's enough! Don't push me too far, Saffron,' he warned grimly. He began to propel her towards his parked car. 'I'm doing my best to keep my temper but it isn't easy. Just get in the car and behave yourself. We don't want any more accidents.'

She glared. 'You're acting as if it was *my* fault!'

He didn't speak until he was behind the wheel, turning the key in the ignition, hands shaking with the fury that consumed him. Then he said coldly, 'It seems to have been very much your fault. The motorist who saw what happened says that you were kissing. No wonder the car went off the road!'

'Kissing . . . !' Saffron was outraged.

'Oh, I don't blame Philip,' he said tautly. 'I've kissed you myself. You're a bewitching little baggage and he *is* a Tregarron.'

'You've got it wrong!' she said fiercely, wounded by the careless dismissal of the impulse that had led him to kiss her on occasions.

'You were seen!' he snapped, his tone implying that she was probably a liar as well as a wanton.

'And if Philip had been *killed* . . .' She broke off at the enormity of his readiness to believe a complete stranger before herself. 'Tried and condemned before I had a chance to say anything in my defence, apparently,' she finished bitterly.

Jarvis shrugged. She turned away her head, biting her lip until it bled, hands locked tightly in her lap, and thus they drove the ten miles to Pethnavick in constrained and angry silence. Saffron stared at the winding black ribbon of road, the looming shapes of trees and hedges and houses illuminated by the car's headlights, and wondered how she had come to fall in love with an arrogant, domineering brute who had no heart at all.

When they reached the dower house he stopped the car and Saffron got out, not a word spoken by either. She turned away and heard the sharp slam of the car door and the sudden acceleration of the engine.

She paused in the porch and rested her hot and aching head against the cool stone of a pillar to watch the receding lights of the car as it headed for the big house. She was a confused jumble of hurt, anger and disbelief and a shamed regret that she'd lost her self-control to the point of actually hitting him in public.

She didn't know how she could ever face him again . . .

Despite Dorothy's concerned protests, she got up early the following morning, put on her uniform and reported for duty. There was nothing wrong with her but an aching heart and a troubled mind—and Meredith was already short-staffed. She would rather be busy than worrying about Philip and fretting about the things that Jarvis had said and obviously believed.

But Meredith wouldn't allow her to go on duty in theatre. The non-urgent cases on Philip's list for that day had been postponed, and the rest would be absorbed by Clay's list. She wouldn't be needed and Meredith advised her to take the day off to get over the shock of the accident.

It was kind and well-meant, but Saffron ignored the advice. Instead, she reported to Bronwen that she was available to work on the ward that day. The Welsh girl looked doubtful but she relented when she saw the bleak misery in Saffron's grey eyes. Whatever the cause, work was an excellent panacea for unhappiness, she knew.

Saffron went along to Delia's room, wondering how she had taken the news about Philip. The accident followed much too soon on the tragedy that had cost her a husband and her own mobility and might be a severe setback.

The bright smile that she mustered for her patient's benefit foundered abruptly when she saw Jarvis in the room. Most unprofessionally, he sat on the bed with an arm about Delia, her fair head on his broad shoulder. Pain shafted in Saffron's breast as she saw the warm tenderness of that embrace and the look of love in his dark eyes.

Then she realised that he was comforting Delia rather than making love to her, and Saffron was vaguely ashamed of her swift and ugly resentment, that would deny a tragic young widow a second chance of happiness. Delia's violet eyes were swimming in tears and her lovely face was hauntingly sad. Perhaps it was too fanciful, but she thought that Delia was like a delicately beautiful flower, crumpled and beaten by wind and rain, scarcely able to survive in a cruel world without support.

No wonder Jarvis wanted to surround her with his love and his protective concern and take care of her for the rest of his life, as he obviously did, Saffron thought bleakly. How could she doubt his love for someone so gentle, so helpless, so feminine and appealing? Had she ever hoped that *she* might mean something to him, one day? She was an awful fool . . .

She hesitated on the threshold of the room, heart hammering in her throat. This was the moment she had been dreading. The moment of meeting Jarvis.

'Well, come in, Nurse Pierce,' he said, brusque and peremptory and unsmiling. 'Perhaps *you* can convince your patient that she isn't a jinx. I'm damned if *I* can!'

Had she really expected a smile, a kind word, some concerned enquiry as to her health or feelings? She might as well wish for the moon, Saffron thought bitterly. She approached the bed, dredging a smile for Delia from the depths of her depression, ignoring the doctor.

'Feeling low?' she said, warmly sympathetic. 'I've a sure cure for that. It's a lovely morning and there's time for a walk along the cliffs before your physiotherapy.'

She might not have spoken. Delia didn't even look at her. As Jarvis withdrew his arm and rose, she clutched at him. 'I *am* a jinx' she declared passionately. 'First Ivor and now Philip!'

'I've told you that Philip is going to be fine,' he said with just a hint of impatience. 'He isn't dead or in any danger of dying, believe me! Nurse Pierce can set your mind at rest on that score.'

'Certainly I can,' she said promptly. 'There's no need to worry about Philip. He'll be up and about in no time.'

'But he's badly hurt, he has to be! The car was a write-off, wasn't it?'

'Now where did you hear such nonsense? There seem to be a lot of silly rumours flying about,' Saffron said with a tiny barb in her tone that was intended for the listening Jarvis. 'I was in the car, too, Delia. Look, I haven't a scratch on me! Philip was just unlucky, that's all.'

'Luckier than Ivor,' Delia retorted, ominously low.

'Within a few days, Philip should be well enough to come home,' Jarvis said briskly, to distract an unhappy train of thought. 'There's an empty room next door and it might be a good idea to put him in it. You can help to keep him amused and encourage him to get well as soon as possible. I think you'll be very good for each other!'

In other circumstances, Saffron might have thought that he approved and furthered his cousin's hopes where Delia was concerned. But Jarvis had his own plans for Delia. He'd lost her briefly to Ivor. There was no way that he'd let her slip through his hands into the arms of yet another man, she felt.

Jarvis glanced at her with a slight lift to his eyebrow. 'Your silence indicates that we are in agreement, Nurse Pierce. A rare event,' he murmured, coldly sardonic.

'It's an excellent idea, of course,' she said, carefully not meeting his eyes. 'A form of mutual therapy that ought to benefit both.'

'Exactly.' Gently, he disengaged Delia's clutching fingers. 'It's time you were out of that bed, and I have some patients waiting for me, you know.' He smiled down at her. 'You forget that I'm a busy man.'

Her lovely mouth suddenly folded into a tight, rebellious line. '*Too* busy, as usual. You never did have enough time for me,' she said with a degree of resentment in her soft voice that Saffron had never heard before. 'That's just why I didn't marry you, Jarvis. Ivor always had time to listen, to be interested, to care. Ivor *really* loved me . . .'

Her voice broke and a solitary tear welled and began to trickle down the delicate curve of the pale cheek. Saffron saw the shadow that crossed the doctor's face and suddenly, foolishly, she felt desperately sorry for him.

He put a hand to that perfect pearl of a tear and wiped it away with a loving and compassionate gesture. Then he bent to kiss her cheek, very tenderly. Like a man very much in love, Saffron thought, pierced by pain.

He went from the room without even a nod or a smile for her, leaving her in absolutely no doubt of his indifference and contempt.

She said stiffly, '*He* loves you, too, Delia.' It was reproach that she couldn't help.

Delia sighed. 'Yes. I'm not very kind to him, I suppose. It isn't fair to compare him with Ivor. But it isn't fair that Ivor had to die, is it? I miss him so much.'

'So does Jarvis, I think. Brothers can be very close.' Saffron felt that it ought not to be necessary to remind Delia that others had also suffered from that tragic accident. She was still so absorbed in her own pain that she had no thought or compassion for the way his family felt about Ivor's death.

'I don't know. They weren't alike, except in looks. Ivor was so easy-going, so full of fun. Everyone liked him. Jarvis doesn't care about being liked and he'll trample over everyone to get what he wants. He's so ruthless.'

Saffron went into the adjoining bathroom to turn on the taps and sprinkle delicately perfumed oil into the water. It wouldn't do to let Delia see how much she disliked the unfair criticism of a man who loved and supported her at every turn.

She no longer believed in the ruthlessness that was attributed to him. She could believe that he spoke his mind without fear or favour and fought hard for what he believed in and for what he wanted. She could believe that he set high standards for everyone, including himself. But cold, unfeeling, selfish? Certainly not where Delia was concerned—and perhaps not at all, despite appearances.

Cast into too-familiar lethargy by the news about Philip, Delia was disinclined to get up and it took a mixture of cajoling and firmness to persuade her first into the prepared bath and then to dress. Saffron found herself surprisingly short of patience for a well-trained nurse. Delia could look just like a hurt child whenever she was forced into something she didn't wish to do. A very successful ploy at times, no doubt, Saffron thought, hardening her heart.

The fragile beauty and enchanting air of helpless femininity meant that Delia had been rather spoiled. Saffron was beginning to wonder if the appeal might be contrived to some extent. An affectation that had always brought the men flocking about her and had also won the tender and protective love of the very man that she claimed to be without a heart!

For the first time, Saffron even wondered if the softness and sweetness could be a cloak for a clever and calculating determination. Girls like herself, capable and strong-willed and independent, were seldom so successful at finding men ready and willing to look after them for the rest of their lives, she thought cynically. Girls like Delia seemed to manage it without apparently trying.

Out of the blue, Delia said abruptly, 'I don't think I *can* marry Jarvis.'

Words and tone implied that she'd been urged to

name a day for their wedding and Saffron's heart quivered with painful shock.

'Then you should tell him so,' she said, her voice carefully light to conceal dismay at his eagerness as well as a hope that Delia *would* refuse him.

'It isn't easy to tell him *anything*,' Delia reminded her, sighing. 'He takes things for granted and implies that he knows better than I do what's best for me. And maybe he does.'

Saffron sympathised with her feelings. He had a very dominant personality and Delia was too timid to protest or challenge his decisions. At the same time, she was impatient that mere weakness could allow Delia to drift into marrying him because it was easier than making a stand or admitting to reluctance.

'You don't have to marry Jarvis or anyone else,' she said firmly, trying to sound dispassionate about something that affected herself so strongly. 'Not for a long time, anyway. You still aren't well enough to be making decisions about your future and frankly I'm surprised that Jarvis seems to be rushing you.'

'He isn't. He never talks about us or the future. But I know it's on his mind. I can sense it—and it makes me feel guilty, remembering what I did and knowing he still loves me. He expects me to marry him in the end. I know he does. And I can't bear to hurt him again, Saffron. He'd be so dreadfully angry, too,' she added unhappily. 'He understood about Ivor—that I couldn't help loving him. But to refuse to marry him for no reason . . .' Delia shook her head sorrowfully. 'I don't see how I *can* do that to him.'

Saffron felt like shaking her. Surely no one would marry a man rather that hurt his feelings or incur his anger! And it wasn't so long since Delia hadn't hesitated to wound him deeply by marrying his brother. It was rather late in the day for her to be so concerned about his feelings.

Then, trying to be fair, she reminded herself that Delia had been through a terrible and traumatic time and was still far from well and still in mourning for Ivor. It was not surprising if she had no heart to care what happened to her and no strength of mind to combat someone as determined as Jarvis.

'I think you should be sure before you agree to anything,' she said rather shortly, settling Delia into her wheelchair with a view to taking her out into the sunshine until the Swedish girl came to whisk her away for further physiotherapy.

'How I envy you,' Delia sighed. 'So sure of yourself and so clever at running your life. You're not afraid of Jarvis, are you? You'd find it easy to say no to him. I wish I could.'

'You find it difficult because you're fond of him,' Saffron returned evasively. As if *she* was not! 'You want to please him. But that isn't a good enough reason for marrying him, you know.'

On an impulse, Saffron bent to hug the girl who she still regarded as friend, despite the love and longing for Jarvis that was beginning to colour her attitudes. 'There may never be another Ivor for you,' she said gently, with understanding. 'But I'm sure there must be someone more suited to you than Jarvis. Please give him a chance to come along.'

It was a more fervent plea than she'd meant it to be, prompted as much by an ardent desire for the smallest chance of happiness for herself as by genuine concern that Delia shouldn't ruin her life by marrying the wrong man. But wrapped in herself, Delia didn't even notice . . .

It was much later that day when Saffron saw Jarvis

again. She was with a patient when he passed by the open door. He glanced into the room but didn't smile or speak and she thought wryly that she had really put herself beyond the pale as far as he was concerned.

She checked pulse and temperature and blood pressure. She changed a dressing, checked the position of a drainage tube and adjusted the flow of a drip, talking quietly and reassuringly all the while to the anxious and disorientated girl who'd shattered a kneecap when she fell from a horse. She made a slight adjustment to the traction weights and finally left the patient feeling much more comfortable in body and mind.

That was what a nurse's job was all about, of course. Saffron was thankful for the training that enabled her to carry out routine nursing procedures and provide tender loving care with her heart in her work even while that same heart was heavy and the future seemed bleak, without even the hope of happiness with a man she loved.

'Nurse Pierce!' Saffron turned at the familiar, peremptory sound.

'Dr Tregarron!' It was a little too quick, mocking the deliberately hurtful formality that was so pointed in such an informal and friendly place as the Tregarron Clinic.

He looked down at her from that impressive height. 'It seems that I owe you an apology,' he said brusquely.

'Several,' she replied tartly.

A smile flickered . . . and fled. It seemed that apologising didn't come easily to Jarvis Tregarron.

'I've seen Philip this afternoon and he's making good progress,' he said abruptly. 'I've also talked to some people who told me more about the accident than I knew last night. Apparently I misunderstood a reference to a kiss.'

'Oh?' Saffron didn't mean to make it any easier for him. She was still smarting, still angry.

'My mind must have been on Philip and I didn't listen carefully to the eye-witness account of what happened. Far from risking his life, it appears that you saved it for him. I'm extremely sorry that I spoke as I did to you.'

It was generous. Saffron forgave him instantly. 'I'm a nurse. I did what came naturally,' she reminded him, smiling.

'My family owe you a debt we can never repay.'

'Please, don't say anything more,' she said quickly, colouring. 'I'm fond of Philip and I'm just thankful that he's all right.'

'He's going to be fine. You did a very good job, as usual.'

Praise from him was too rare. Saffron looked up at him swiftly, suspicious of the warmth in his deep voice. 'Thank you.'

'Despite our differences, I do appreciate your many good qualities, Saffron,' he went on with a sudden, disarming smile. 'I should be sorry if you left because of anything I've said or done.'

Their eyes met and held. How easily he could make her melt! He didn't even have to touch her for her heart to quicken and the tide of excitement to flow in her veins!

Something sparked between them and she knew that he was consumed with similar feelings. If only they were the right feelings, she thought wistfully. If only he cared as she did. But he wanted her for all the wrong reasons and love was the last thing that he had in mind where she was concerned. Love was for Delia. She could be no more than another conquest for a sensual man if she yielded to the desire that lit twin flames of fire in the depths of his dark eyes.

'This is a sudden change of heart,' she said rather too brightly, clinging to her pride.

He frowned. 'I think you've always known perfectly well how I feel about you, Saffron,' he said roughly. 'Nothing's changed. I still want you. Surely we can be friends, at least? You get on well enough with everyone else—Clay, Philip, Tom van Wyk . . .'

It wasn't possible that he was jealous! That he really did care! Her heart stood still but Saffron didn't dare to believe all that was in his eyes and voice, and she was too proud to let him know too soon how much it meant to her that he should care. Floundering slightly, she took refuge in a little foolish flippancy.

'Then maybe I've as many friends as I need, Dr Tregarron,' she said, teasing him gently.

Too late, she realised that it hadn't been easy for him to swallow his pride and reach out for her, and that he was in no mood to be teased. Too late, she knew her mistake as he abruptly turned on his heel and strode away from her . . .

CHAPTER THIRTEEN

BLANKET-BATHING a patient gave Saffron plenty of time to review that encounter with Jarvis and realise how badly she'd handled the offer of an olive-branch from such a proud and passionate man.

But she didn't regret her refusal to fall into his arms just at the beckoning of his finger. She was quite determined not to give him the sexual satisfaction that she still felt was all he wanted from her. If she didn't love him so much, she might weaken and yield to her own flame of longing for him. But, loving him, she couldn't be content with so little. Half a loaf was *not* better than none at all. She wanted all or nothing where Jarvis was concerned And it seemed that nothing was precisely what she would get . . .

It didn't help matters when he walked into Bronwen's office less than an hour later to find her in Clay Tregarron's arms!

Clay's admiration and open pursuit had rapidly become a joke that she shared with Bronwen, who'd also suffered from his attentions in the past. He seemed deaf to snubs, blind to distaste and impervious to the amusement that they'd decided might be an effective way of keeping him at bay.

Saffron had come to accept his absurd compliments and frequent attempts at flirtation as a mild irritation that was all part of the day's work. So maybe she was too relaxed, too little on her guard, when he found her alone in the office.

'There you are!' he declared as warmly as if he'd

searched high and low to find her that afternoon. 'How are you now? Any ill effects from the crash?'

Saffron was checking the contents of the drugs cupboard. With her mind on what she was doing, and rather touched by a concern that had been lacking in his cousin, she looked round at the surgeon with a brighter smile than usual. 'Oh, I'm fine, thanks. Just a bruise or two, that's all.'

'I hear you had a bump on the head.' He closed the door and moved further into the room. 'Let's have a look at it.'

'Nothing to see,' she assured him hastily.

'At least I can kiss it better,' he said softly, moving closer. As sure of himself as all the Tregarrons, he took her into his arms in one swift movement.

She was about to thrust him away indignantly when Jarvis opened the door and looked in, obviously expecting to find Bronwen at her desk. He checked an exclamation that was as contemptuous as it was angry.

Clay let her go immediately. 'Caught in the act,' he declared with a light, unrepentant laugh. 'No need to look so disapproving, Jarvis. You know I'm not the man to turn down a tempting offer!'

Saffron could have killed him for the implication that she'd invited and welcomed that ardent embrace. She promptly opened her mouth to protest, to set the record straight, but Jarvis didn't give her the chance to say anything.

With a kind of weary resignation in his eyes and voice, he drawled, 'I wish you'd meet your women elsewhere, Clay—and in their time rather than mine. I don't pay these nurses to aid and abet you in your extra-marital indulgences.' A scornful curl of the lip, a glance that raked poor Saffron with cold contempt, and then Jarvis walked from the office, leaving the door open in very pointed manner.

Flushed and furious, hurt and humiliated by the deliberate sneer and the insulting sweep of those dark eyes, Saffron turned on the surgeon, eyes blazing and voice shaking with anger.

'What a bloody menace you are!' she flared. 'You think you're God's gift to women, don't you? Well, you're not—and I'm fed up with the way you sneak round me like an oversexed tom cat! Keep away from me—and you can tell that damn cousin of yours that I'm *not* one of your women, in his time or my own!'

She'd never been so angry—or so frightened, for it was so terribly important that Jarvis shouldn't think any more ill of her at this point. They'd been so near to a new and better understanding until her foolish tongue had let her down again.

Clay had the grace to look abashed at first, but he swiftly rallied and his eyes narrowed with sudden, glinting suspicion and a dangerous amusement.

'Care what Jarvis thinks, do you?' he mocked. 'Fancy him, do you? Don't waste your time, my sweet. He only has eyes for Delia. So why not settle for me? There's not much to choose between us, after all. Close your eyes and you won't know which of us is making love to you, I promise.'

For the second time in two days, Saffron hit a Tregarron, her hand landing on his cheek with a very satisfactory sound. His head jerked back with the shock and the force of the blow and she saw the red marks of her angry fingers across his handsome face.

'You'll regret that,' he said softly, grimly.

'Oh, go to hell!' Saffron could hear Jarvis and Bronwen talking in the corridor and she wondered bitterly why it hadn't been her friend who'd burst in on them, coming to her rescue. Did it have to be Jarvis, who probably believed that she'd given his amorous cousin every encouragement to make love to her behind a closed door?

Clay narrowly missed colliding with Bronwen in the doorway as he swung out of the room with a look on his sensually handsome face that promised trouble in the very near future.

Saffron wondered if he had sufficient influence or authority to have her dismissed. Jarvis might be thankful to have a reason to be rid of her, she thought bleakly— and then told herself defiantly that she'd be glad to see the back of the Tregarron Clinic *and* the Tregarrons.

Bronwen looked after the surgeon with dislike in her brown eyes. Then she smiled at Saffron with sympathy. Treated to an unavoidable earful of the exchange between nurse and surgeon, both she and Jarvis had been carefully deaf to everything but their own brief conversation. There hadn't been the slightest flicker of reaction in the doctor's dark eyes. But she'd dearly love to be a fly on the wall when he next encountered his insufferable cousin, Bronwen thought dryly.

'You're upset, girl,' she said gently, noting tension in Saffron's slight figure and distress in the grey eyes. 'I could slap that old nuisance myself, indeed!'

Saffron knew there was no need for pretence. That slap and the angry words must have echoed through the building! 'I'm afraid I lost my temper . . .'

'Only way with some of them, isn't it? He'll have a hard old time of it explaining that face to Meredith. Serve him right,' Bronwen said with obvious satisfaction.

Saffron managed to smile. Gradually she regained her composure and her sense of proportion. Shortly before she went off duty, Clay came back, stiff and slightly

shamefaced but apparently sincere, to offer an apology.
She didn't think she could ever forgive him, remembering the way that Jarvis had looked and spoken and
thinking of the damage that had been done to a fractionally improving relationship. But she accepted the
apology with a reasonably good grace.

Several of the staff were away with the flu and Saffron
spent a busy week, working all hours to help out in
Theatre or on other wards. Philip was brought from the
hospital in Helston later in the week and duly installed in
the room next to Delia, and Saffron helped to nurse him
whenever she worked on the orthopaedic ward. He was
already making progress towards a full recovery and his
needs had proved to be an incentive to Delia to do some
things for him and more for herself, just as Jarvis had
predicted. Hadn't he also realised that proximity and a
growing affection for each other would eventually pose
a threat to his own hopes for the future? Saffron
wondered.

Having worked through a weekend and a long week
with scarcely a break and no word of approval from a
stiff, chilly and very distant doctor, Saffron went off duty
earlier than usual on the following Friday with a whole
weekend to herself at last. Longing to get away from
the clinic and all its painful reminders, she settled for the
beach. For someone who loved the sea and the sun,
she'd had little time to enjoy either since her arrival at
Pethnavick.

She walked for some distance, clambering over rocks,
until she came to a small and secluded cove. It was a very
hot afternoon and she took off her thin shirt and jeans
to sunbathe in a brief white bikini. With her beach-bag
as a pillow, she lay down on the warm sand, trying to
relax, trying to close her mind to all thought of Jarvis

Tregarron. Being busy had helped to some extent, but it seemed that she was as hopelessly in love with him as ever . . .

She didn't know how long she slept in the hot sun, but she woke to find that the incoming tide was starting to encroach on the small cove, which lay between two ramparts of rock. A sleek blue and white cabin cruiser was moving smoothly in the direction of Penzance, a hundred yards out to sea.

Saffron sat up, hugging her knees, wondering if Jarvis was alone and where he was going. There was so much of his life that was a closed book to her—and so much of his future that she would never share, she thought sadly.

He sailed indifferently on his way, seeming to be unaware of the girl on the beach, a diminutive figure against the craggy majesty of the cliff and the rocks that grovelled at its hem.

As the boat rounded the headland, Saffron moved her clothes further up the beach, nearer to the cliff, and then went to cool off and forget about Jarvis in the welcoming sea. It was colder than she'd expected, whisking her breath away as she plunged into the waves. There was a stronger current than she'd expected, too, tugging at her legs and body. The tide was coming in quickly and strongly and she swam back to the safety of the shore.

She clambered on to the low string of rocks and settled herself comfortably to dry off in the sunshine, to enjoy the swell of sparkling and dancing waves and to watch, albeit unconciously, for the return of the cruiser.

She sat for a long time, lost in dreams, intently watching the horizon while the tide came in with a rush, swirling round the rocks, sweeping into the cove and out again and taking her forgotten and unnoticed jeans, shirt and bag with it.

When Saffron eventually roused from her reverie at

the welcome sight of the returning sailor, she found that she was surrounded by sea and that the water was steadily inching higher about the rock where she was perched. The cove was filled with tumbling, foaming water. Her heart failed her although she was no coward. For she abruptly realised that the rocks were probably covered at high tide and that the cliff rose sharply and sheerly behind her. And she wasn't a strong enough swimmer to combat the current if she tried to swim along to an uncovered stretch of the shore.

She hadn't made sufficient allowance for the unknown behaviour of the tides along this coast, despite the fact that Jarvis had warned her about them days before. She stood up slowly, stiff from salt and sun and sitting, and watched the alarmingly slow approach of the boat as it made its way back to its usual mooring. Would Jarvis see and hear her if she waved and shouted? More important, would he be near enough to hail before she lost her increasingly precarious footing and tumbled into the sea which seemed to be only waiting to sweep her away and dash her against the jagged rocks with all the force of its unexpected fury?

She was a fool—and she might be a dead fool if Jarvis didn't come to her rescue very soon, Saffron thought with a little panic rising in her breast. She might be safer sitting than standing, even if the sea did swirl about her—but how could he possibly see her if she merged with the contours of the rocks?

So she knelt instead on the painfully sharp surface and waved both arms above her head in a desperate effort to attract his attention, while the sea spitefully leaped higher to splash her face and sparkle on her tumbled hair in the sunshine. She shouted, scarcely able to hear her own voice above the slap of the water and despairing that Jarvis would hear it at all.

The boat drew nearer. Saffron stood with the sea clutching at her ankles and waved more furiously and shouted more loudly. Past caring about anything but rescue, she took off the white bikini top and flapped it wildly in the breeze, hoping it would catch his eye more readily than her waving arms. And then she saw Jarvis move suddenly to the side of the cruiser, leaning to stare intently in her direction before he waved to show that he'd seen her and turned away to change course and increase speed. The freshening wind suddenly whipped the bikini bra from her hand and carried it out to sea, but it had served her purpose and Saffron watched it dancing on the waves without regret.

The cruiser came to a halt some distance away and Jarvis tossed the anchor overboard while Saffron watched and waited, wondering if he expected her to swim the short but frightening expanse of water that divided them.

'The current's too strong!' she shouted.

He nodded, understanding. 'I'm coming to you. Just stay there!'

'I'm not planning to go anywhere,' she said wryly, beneath her breath, watching as he unfastened the dinghy and then lowered himself over the side and dropped into it.

'Hang on!' he shouted reassuringly, beginning to row towards her with sure and powerful strokes.

Saffron took the advice quite literally. She crouched, clinging with both hands to sharply jutting crags to save herself from slipping into the churning sea. She was terrified for herself and for him as the small boat was swept to and fro by the current and seemed as if it might founder at any moment on unseen rocks below the surface of the water.

Then he reached her and stretched out for her with

strong hands and lifted her into the dinghy. She clung to him, tears streaming down her cheeks, saying his name over and over again in relief and reaction and a wealth of loving.

Jarvis held her close, crushed against his heart, his cheek pressed hard to her soft, bright, spray-drenched hair.

'It's all right,' he said softly. 'It's all right, my dear love . . .' She *was* dear to him, very precious, and he couldn't bear to think how nearly she might have been lost to him, utterly and for ever.

He knew this coast and its treacherous tides and currents as she did not. The pride that had kept him from his happiness with this girl would have been cold comfort it she'd drowned, he realised.

'Oh, Jarvis . . .' Saffron was shivering from shock and anxiety and the very nearness of him, and she thought she must have imagined the tenderness and the meaning of those murmured words.

'Panic over—you're safe,' he told her, soothingly, reassuringly. 'I'm looking after you now.' He held her away slightly, urging her to sit down on the wooden seat in the bow. Her hands clung tightly, reluctant to release him. He smiled down at her, very tender. 'Careful—don't capsize us,' he warned lightly. 'Let's get into calmer waters with rather more deck beneath our feet and then you can cling to me as much as you like!'

Saffron smiled tremulously in response to the teasing words that made light of the anxiety she suddenly knew that he'd felt during those desperate moments. Her heart lifted with a new hope that she meant more to him than she'd ever dared to dream.

She sat down, facing him and, suddenly shy and self-conscious, folded her arms across her bare breasts, hugging herself for warmth as well as modesty. Without comment, Jarvis took off his shirt and handed it to her, as casually as if he was unaware of her near-nudity, and then took up the oars. Saffron gratefully slipped her arms into the sleeves of the shirt and drew it about her, but her hands trembled too much from cold and reaction to fasten the buttons.

He helped her to climb on board the cruiser and then jerked his dark head towards the cabin. 'You'll find some towels inside. Wrap up warmly while I secure the dinghy.'

She was curled on a bunk when he entered, a huge towel gathered closely about her slight body. She was shivering, unable to control the rigor, but she managed a small smile for him. His heart wrenched as he saw the small feet peeping from the edge of the towel, torn and bleeding slightly from the cruel rocks. He wanted to cradle them in his hands and kiss them. He wanted to take her into his arms and warm her with the heat of his own body and the flame of the desire that had mounted steadily since their first meeting, unquenched by pride or battle or seeming futility.

'I'm having a bad attack of reaction,' she said apologetically. 'That was a bit scary.'

'You don't know this coast. It can play some dangerous tricks.' Jarvis went to a cupboard and took out a bottle and glasses. He poured a generous amount of brandy into a glass and held it out to her. 'This is what you need.'

Saffron looked at the glass and then at him, doubtful. 'I've no head for spirits, Jarvis. It will probably make me drunk.'

'I'll look after you if it does,' he told her lightly. 'And don't tell me that you can take care of yourself, will you? Not after today's episode.' It was gently teasing and his smile was very warm.

'You don't know how glad I was to see you!'

'Any port in a storm?' he asked. He stood over her while she reluctantly swallowed most of the potent brandy. 'Relax and keep warm. I'll make coffee.'

Saffron watched him as he moved about the galley, busy with coffee-pot and mugs, the muscles rippling in his bronzed back and shoulders and powerful chest. The warm glow of the brandy in the pit of her stomach began to trickle steadily through her veins and light a little fire in the secret places of her body.

Relaxing, warm, hugging the memory of words that she scarcely dared to believe he'd spoken, let alone meant, she began to ache for him in a way that complemented the continual ache of love and longing that filled her heart.

Jarvis glanced at her with a slow, sensual smile that instantly flooded her with wanting. 'Feeling better?'

'Feeling fine . . .' She moistened dry lips. Her heart pounded and her whole body tingled and she wished she had the courage to hold out her arms to him, knowing that he was too sensual to refuse what she was longing to give in return for the comfort of his embrace.

He turned back to his task, waiting for the coffee to percolate, separated from her by a few yards that seemed a hundred miles to Saffron. She looked at the proud head, the strong column of his neck and the broad shoulders and deeply tanned back, the contrasting white of his flesh where the brief denim shorts began. He was very male, very attractive—and she loved him very much.

She moved swiftly, silently, sliding her arms about him and pressing her face to his shoulder. He stiffened and her heart shook with the fear that he meant to reject her.

'Let me hold you . . .' Her arms tightened abruptly about him.

For a moment, he stood very still. Then he turned in her arms to look intently into her eyes, a slight smile in his own.

'The brandy? Or gratitude?' he asked, gently mocking the unexpected overture from the girl who'd kept him so sternly at arm's length for days. He put his hands on her shoulders, closing them on her soft flesh, drawing her against him.

'Must it be either?' she asked softly.

'It has to be for real,' he told her, a roughness in his deep voice as desire dragged heavily at his loins. 'Don't play games with me, Saffron. I want you too much.'

With a sigh, she reached to kiss him. Her lips were soft, warm, telling him all that he needed to know. He pulled her body into his own, forcing her to abrupt awareness of the hotly-throbbing passion that she'd stirred in him. He kissed her, long and deep, compelling her to response and she melted in his arms, eager for the power and the glory of his lovemaking.

Abruptly, he swung her up into his arms, his lips warm against her own, and carried her back to the bunk. He laid her down on the cushions and looked at her with a little smile in the depths of his eyes, his lean body trembling with the force of his love and desire.

'There's no going back, Saffron,' he warned, low and tense. 'I'm taking you all the way unless you stop me now. I won't give you another chance to change your mind.'

Unafraid, Saffron smiled at him with her heart in her eyes. She loved him and she wanted him. Heart and body belonged to him by the dictates of destiny, come what may.

'You promised me fireworks,' she reminded him very

softly, and slid her arms up and about his neck to draw him down to her side.

She gave herself up to delight as his strong hands found her breasts, cradling and caressing and sending swift shafts of pleasure into the deepest centre of her being, moving over her slight body in slow and sensuous strokes that grew steadily more intimate and more exciting, flooding her with a delicious languor and an ever greater desire to cross the last threshold between virginity and fulfilled womanhood.

The boat rocked gently to the turn of the tide as he urged her towards the sighing sweetness of the final surrender. Skilfully, sensitive to her smallest response, he took her closer to ecstasy with every brush of his lips on face and hair and body, every flickering touch of his expert hands, heightening her first sexual experience with the incredible magic of his tender understanding of her needs. Fiercely ardent, strongly sensual, he was the most tender and caring of lovers as he carried her with him to the peaks of mutual and glorious culmination . . .

CHAPTER FOURTEEN

THE LAST rays of the setting sun caught the glints of gold in her hair as the dinghy reached the shore. Saffron stepped out to the wet sand and caught her foot, stumbling slightly. Jarvis moved quickly to catch her and looked down at her with a twinkle in the dark eyes.

'So it *was* the brandy!'

'Not at all. You saved my life,' she reminded him demurely, laughter lurking in the grey eyes.

'Then it was gratitude.'

'Don't embarrass me,' she said lightly. She smiled at him. 'You know perfectly well that I just couldn't resist you any longer, Dr Tregarron.'

He drew her close, his heart thudding heavily against her breast. 'Don't ever call me that again! It turns me into a stranger,' he told her tensely.

Saffron clung to him wordlessly, desperately afraid that it would all end with their return to reality. For the Tregarron Clinic was waiting for them with all its demands that divided their lives.

My dear love, he'd surely said, rescuing her from the rocks—and not another word of love to quieten her anxious heart, for all the ardour of his lovemaking.

She couldn't believe that she meant nothing at all to him, not now. But he was so proud, so determined—and if he'd made up his mind to prove to the world that he could marry Delia then he might not allow his feeling for another woman to stand in the way. Tregarron pride might be stronger than Jarvis Tregarron's desire for this wilful and spirited nurse who'd challenged him at every turn for weeks and finally thrown herself into his arms with wanton abandon.

Men fought to marry the Delias of this world, it seemed. Girls like herself seemed to be regarded as potential lovers rather than possible wives . . .

Her silence troubled him. 'Regrets?' he asked quietly.

She smiled in swift reassurance. 'No.' Only for the murmured *I love you* that had spilled from the depths of her being on the crest of glory, she thought wryly—and only because there had been no murmur of reassuring response from the man who shared the golden and unforgettable moment.

'Sure? I know it was the first time for you, Saffron,' he said gently. 'Why on earth did you come at me as if you knew what it was all about?'

She blushed, remembering. 'Sheer desperation,' she said lightly. As if it wasn't the absolute truth.

He laughed. 'I know the feeling! Wanting you has been torment all these weeks. Making love to you was just as wonderful as I always knew it would be . . .' He stroked the curve of her cheek, outlined her mouth with fleeting fingers and then followed the tender tracing with his lips in a lover's kiss. 'I shall be making love to you for a very long time,' he told her firmly, confidently, claiming her for his own.

In any other man, that kiss and those words might be evidence of love, Saffron thought wistfully. But she suspected that it was only the afterglow of sexual delight in his case. She had pleased and delighted him and he assumed with characteristic arrogance that she would be willing to please him in like manner for as long as it suited him to want her. But she loved him too much to mind.

His hand briefly cradled her head and then he put her

away, almost abruptly, and turned to drag the dinghy along the beach to its mooring ring.

Saffron followed gingerly, conscious of her sore feet, although he'd bathed them tenderly and treated them with ointment and found her a pair of socks. They were much too big but she wore them happily because they belonged to him, like the shirt that she wore over the still-damp bikini briefs.

Jarvis came back for her and swung her up into his arms and carried her across the sand. She realised his strength, his fitness, as he climbed the path to the top of the cliff with her in his arms, making light of its steep ascent and her weight.

Her arm tightened about his neck and she touched her lips to his cheek, wondering if they would ever again know the closeness that seemed to bind them. At that moment, secure in his strong arms, remembering the enchanted idyll that they'd briefly created for each other, she could almost believe that he loved her and that they had a future together. Then the gabled roof of the Tregarron Clinic came into view, reminding her poignantly of Delia's importance and her own uncertain place in his life.

She didn't even know when she would see him again, or in what circumstances. For he was going to London to attend a medical conference and would be away for some days and she had no confidence at all in the way he would feel about her on his return.

'I'll find my own way from here, Jarvis,' she said abruptly. 'If we're seen together, with me looking like a shipwrecked mariner in your socks and shirt, people will think all kinds of things.'

'And they'll be right,' he laughed, dark eyes twinkling as he set her down.

'Yes . . .' Saffron suddenly found it hard to smile, to

be light-hearted about something that she might yet have cause to regret. She looked up at him a little anxiously. 'There's no need to tell anyone what happened, is there? We don't want to worry anyone and I'm perfectly all right, thanks to you.'

'If you hadn't been, I should have begun to believe in Delia's jinx,' he told her grimly, wondering if she had any idea how much she meant to him. He loved her and soon he would tell her so, ask her to marry him. But not at a moment when she might suppose that the words resulted from a spontaneous and satisfying encounter rather than a real and lasting love. He had to find a way to convince her.

The name hung heavily between them and Saffron felt as though a hand had suddenly and brutally squeezed her heart.

Jarvis took her face in his two hands and kissed her. Then he said sternly, 'No more prickles. Too much time has been wasted in fighting each other, Saffron. Things must be different in future.'

'Yes, Doctor,' she said, mock demure, grey eyes laughing at him. 'I will be good, Doctor.'

He smiled, shook his head. 'I don't think you know how to be! That streak of independence is as inbred in you as pride is in me, I'm afraid. Heaven knows how you survived three years of hospital discipline and etiquette to get your badge!'

'*You* never worked at Kit's,' she said.

'So I'm the villain of the piece! None of it was your fault, I suppose!'

'Yes, it was,' she admitted impulsively, frankly. 'I *have* been prickly. I *haven't* made it easy for you to like me . . .'

'Liking is one thing. The way I feel about you is something else. Nothing's changed,' he said warmly, reassuring her. 'I still want you . . . more than ever.'

Her heart shook. 'I'm glad.' She smiled at him, trying not to mind too much that he spoke of wanting and never loving.

Jarvis hesitated. Then he said quietly, 'You said that you love me, Saffron. I need to know if it's true.'

Her heart leaped like a wild thing in her breast but the look in his eyes and her own honesty made it quite impossible for her to lie to him. And why should she lie? There was no wrong in loving. The wrong would be in denying the prompting of her heart.

'Yes.' She met the intent dark eyes without flinching. 'I think I've always loved you.'

He nodded, satisfied. 'Then trust me. I won't allow anyone or anything to hurt you.' He kissed her again, very tenderly, the touch of his lips setting a seal on the words . . .

While he was in London, Saffron had plenty of time to reflect on the words with their hint of promise and wonder just how much, if anything, he'd really meant by them. She had time to recall that traumatic experience on the rocks with the threatening sea surrounding her and the skilled and sensual lovemaking that had followed her rescue. And she had too much time to remember that she'd believed from the beginning that he was deeply in love with Delia and felt only a strong sexual desire for herself.

Perhaps it was foolish to look for a letter, to hope for a telephone call. He wasn't that kind of man, she reminded herself. He was a dedicated and single-minded doctor and no doubt the medical conference had pushed all thought of her into the background.

At least he would be back in time for Delia's twenty-fifth birthday and the family dinner party that had been arranged in celebration of the event. Saffron was invited but she didn't expect anyone to remember that it was also her birthday and she had a sinking feeling that she wouldn't have any cause for celebration.

For Delia seemed to be hugging a secret of some kind to her breast. She was as excited as a child about the evening ahead when Saffron reported for duty at her usual hour, birthday or no birthday, and she seemed a different person to the frail and unhappy widow of a few weeks before.

Saffron tried not to mind that there had been no card from Jarvis, although almost everyone else had remembered and several small gifts were pressed upon her by friends she'd made since coming to Pethnavick. She was much more disappointed by his failure to return from the London conference.

However, Delia was confident that he would arrive in good time for the dinner party. 'He has a very special reason to be here,' she assured Saffron with sparkling eyes. She put a finger mischievously to her lips. 'I mustn't say another word, I promised Jarvis! But I can tell you that a lot of people are going to be very surprised tonight. Including you . . . !'

Saffron dropped a thermometer and heard it break, spilling a cascade of silver mercury across the floor. She stooped to gather up the slivers of glass, thankful for an excuse to hide her face and cope with her shocked emotions.

She was utterly dismayed by the hint that Jarvis and Delia intended to make an announcement of some kind that evening. She'd been lulled into a false sense of security by Delia's growing intimacy with Philip, she realised. She'd really believed the danger that Delia would agree to marry Jarvis was a thing of the past. But it needed little intelligence to guess what was in the air, she thought bleakly—and Delia deceived herself if she really supposed that anyone would be surprised by the news that they were going to be married, after all.

Trust me, he'd said. *I won't allow you to be hurt* . . .

But she *was* hurt—to the very core of her being. For he'd taken what he wanted and walked away, knowing that she loved him but still determined to marry Delia. He'd allowed her to hope that he meant all that was in his eyes, his voice and that ardent embrace—and it had apparently been nothing but lies, she thought bitterly.

Hurt! It was like a little death. The sudden collapse of a lovely and foolish dream that she'd been cherishing ever since he'd left her with that kiss and the quiet and apparently meaningful promise of his words.

Saffron straightened, pride keeping back the pain that suffused her entire being. 'I don't think I can make the party tonight, after all,' she said carefully. 'It *is* a family affair and you won't need me there and Bronwen wants me to go out with her and some friends.'

Delia stared. 'But you can't do that! You must be there! You promised!' she said urgently. 'It's *your* party, too. You can't possibly disappoint everyone at the last moment!'

Saffron doubted if anyone would be disappointed or even notice her absence. But she was forced to yield, to assure Delia that she would be there, despite her dread and her heaviness of heart. Delia was so persistent, so near to tears, so desperately anxious, that Saffron couldn't risk upsetting her patient by thwarting her on something which seemed to matter so much. It ought to be heart-warming that Delia was apparently so fond of her and so sure that she would delight in her new-found happiness. As she would if it was any man but Jarvis . . .

The day passed without sight or sound of the dark-haired doctor but Saffron caught sight of his car turning into the gates as she made her way back to the dower house just after four o'clock. Her heart flew into her throat but he drove past her as though he didn't see her—or didn't wish to see her.

She was dreading the dinner-party that seemed to have been planned with more than a birthday celebration in mind. But she dressed in the dark blue taffeta with its square neckline and distinctive puffed sleeves that was her birthday present to herself, arranged her hair in a knot of curls and carefully made up her eyes, determined to put a brave face on the situation. She would prove that Tregarrons didn't hold the monopoly on pride, she told herself firmly.

It was certainly a gathering of the clan, she realised, accepting a drink and a birthday kiss from Clay and turning thankfully to Meredith who drew her down to a sofa with friendly warmth.

Dr Ben still looked very frail but he came across the room to join the two girls and sat down with them, courteously asking Saffron how she was enjoying her work in the clinic and if she'd suffered any ill effects from the accident that had injured Philip. He pressed her hand warmly when she assured him that she was very happy and perfectly well.

Delia and Philip had arrived together. She was animated and lovely in yellow silk, still bubbling with inner excitement, and delighted to have surprised everyone by walking into the room. Philip was in a wheelchair, his leg still in plaster and the strain of the accident still showing slightly in his good-looking face, but he was obviously thankful to be well enough to be present on a family occasion.

Noticing the way that the surgeon's eyes rested on the beautiful and sparkling Delia, Saffron wondered what he would feel that evening when she announced her impending marriage to another man. Perhaps Jarvis deserved to regain his bride, but his happiness would mean heartache for more than one person in that room, Saffron thought heavily.

Fern Tregarron sat quietly in a corner, sipping sherry and observing the scene with a hint of dry amusement in her dark eyes. She was a very attractive girl but she was so reserved and so distant in her attitude to someone she obviously regarded as just another of the clinic nurses that Saffron found it hard to like her. But she reminded herself fairly that she had felt the same way about another Tregarron in the early days . . .

He was missing from the family group. Called out to the eccentric Lady Elizabeth as soon as he'd set foot in the place, Clay explained casually, but Jarvis would join them as soon as he'd changed. They'd wait dinner for him, of course.

Saffron's heart told her when he walked into the room although she stood by the window, talking to Delia. She forced herself to turn to look at him, pride and scorn all ready to leap in defence of that foolish heart.

Their eyes met and held across the big room. He strode towards her—or was it Delia who drew him? Beautiful and appealing and obviously dear to him, the woman he'd lost only briefly to his brother.

Her heart gave a great bound as she realised that the smile in his dark eyes was for herself and that he seemed utterly oblivious to Delia, who tactfully drew back as he reached Saffron's side.

Her heart began to hammer and her legs turned suddenly to jelly as a wild hope soared at the look in his eyes, which seemed to hold all the love and reassurance that any woman could want for her happiness.

'Saffron . . .' Her name was an endearment. He put an arm about her and bent his dark head to kiss her in full

view of his family. 'Happy birthday, my dear love,' he
said for everyone to hear. It was a public declaration so
out of character for a man like Jarvis Tregarron that she
instinctively knew that he meant to convince her and his
family that he was very much in love and totally sure of
what he wanted.

'Oh, Jarvis . . .' She smiled at him shakily, clung to
him, utterly bewildered and gloriously happy and still
not daring to believe.

He took a small, square box from a pocket. 'Here's
your present, darling. I'm sorry it's a bit late.'

'A present?' Saffron looked at him, surprised. What
more could she want than the gift of his love? She
glanced round the room at his family and saw the smiling
satisfaction in Dr Ben's dark eyes as they rested on his
son and herself. She saw Philip's smile of approval and
the way that he reached for Delia's hand as though he
was staking his own claim to happiness. She saw the
dancing delight at her astonishment in Delia's eyes and
knew that she had no need to worry about her reaction.
Delia was no longer a rival for Jarvis' love—and perhaps
she never had been.

There was a slightly wry smile in Clay's dark eyes, a
hint of relief as well as pleasure in Meredith's friendly
nod, indulgent amusement in Fern's expression and a
blessing in the warm smile that the kindly Mary Bellamy
bestowed on them both. Saffron suddenly knew that she
was almost the last person to know just what Jarvis had
planned and she could have shaken him.

'How could you do this to me?' she demanded, torn
between exasperation, thankful relief and an overwhelming love. 'Do you know what I've been through
since I saw you? Days without a word—and now this!
Wretch!'

He smiled, understanding but unrepentant, and gave

her a little hug. 'I told you to trust me. Open your present, Saffron.'

Slowly, almost holding her breath, she lifted the lid of the little box and stared in wide-eyed astonishment and incredulous delight at the beauty of the matching rings that gleamed on the velvet cushion.

A square-cut sapphire and a wide gold band winked at her in the rays of the setting sun as it slanted through the long window. Engagement and wedding rings. More than a welcome birthday present from the man she loved with all her heart and had never really dared to believe could love her in return.

'They're beautiful,' she said softly, shaken, looking up at him with grey eyes luminous and questioning. 'But why? How? I mean—I don't understand, Jarvis.' She was bewildered, confused, almost afraid to believe the implication of the lovely rings and the way he held her against him, smiling at her with a wealth of love and longing in the deep-set, expressive eyes.

He lifted the engagement ring from its bed and reached for her left hand. 'Of course you do,' he told her firmly, sliding the sapphire on to her finger with a smile of satisfaction when he found that it fitted. 'You're going to marry me, Saffron. Tomorrow, in fact. I've a special licence in my pocket and all the arrangements are made.'

It was so cool, so confident—and so like him, Saffron thought, helpless with loving and totally unable to resist this man's will and desire and forceful personality.

It was impossible to declare that she should have been asked, consulted, allowed to plan her own wedding. Having fallen deeply and irrevocably in love with the arrogant Dr Jarvis Tregarron, she must expect to fall in with his wishes without protest. He was so sure that he knew what was best for her—and maybe he did . . .

'Just like that,' she said, half-laughing.

He nodded. 'We love each other and we're right for each other and I can't think of anything better than spending the rest of my life with you,' he said simply.

Saffron's whole being moved with love for him. 'I want to marry you, Jarvis,' she said quietly, carefully, meaning it with all her heart. 'Of course I do! But in such a hurry . . . ?' She felt that she had to make some small protest to assert the last of her independence.

He brushed it aside. 'I'm not giving another woman the chance to change her mind,' he said, the glow in his eyes taking the sting from the blunt words. 'I can't afford to lose *you*—now or ever!' Abruptly, he drew her into an embrace that paid no heed at all to the presence of his family, who tactfully turned back to their drinks, their conversations, their own affairs. 'You fill my heart and mind with loving.' He said it softly, like a prayer.

Only Saffron heard the quiet, heartfelt words, a vow that she would treasure far more than any he made on the following day. Yielding to the will that only wanted her happiness until the end of time, she lifted her face for his kiss.

There might be many times when a wilful and spirited nurse would long to throw something at the handsome dark head of the doctor that she'd married, but Saffron knew that she would never regret that she'd given her heart to him even before she knew that it would be welcome . . .

Doctor Nurse Romances

Romance in modern medical life

Read more about the lives and loves of doctors and nurses in the fascinatingly different backgrounds of contemporary medicine. These are the four Doctor Nurse romances to look out for next month.

NURSE WESTON'S NEW JOB
Clare Lavenham

CANDLES FOR THE SURGEON
Helen Upshall

THE RELUCTANT ANGEL
Sarah Franklin

NURSE ON NEURO
Ann Jennings

Buy them from your usual paperback stockist, or write to: Mills & Boon Reader Service, P.O. Box 236, Thornton Rd, Croydon, Surrey CR9 3RU, England. Readers in South Africa write to: Mills & Boon Reader Service of Southern Africa, Private Bag X3010, Randburg, 2125.

Mills & Boon
the rose of romance

Mills & Boon

4 Doctor Nurse Romances
FREE

Coping with the daily tragedies and ordeals of a busy hospital, and sharing the satisfaction of a difficult job well done, people find themselves unexpectedly drawn together. Mills & Boon Doctor Nurse Romances capture perfectly the excitement, the intrigue and the emotions of modern medicine, that so often lead to overwhelming and blissful love. By becoming a regular reader of Mills & Boon Doctor Nurse Romances you can enjoy EIGHT superb new titles every two months plus a whole range of special benefits: your very own personal membership card, a free newsletter packed with recipes, competitions, bargain book offers, plus big cash savings.

**AND an Introductory FREE GIFT for YOU.
Turn over the page for details.**

**Fill in and send this coupon back today
and we'll send you
4 Introductory
Doctor Nurse Romances yours to keep**

FREE

At the same time we will reserve a
subscription to Mills & Boon
Doctor Nurse Romances for you. Every
two months you will receive the latest
8 new titles, delivered direct to your door.
You don't pay extra for delivery. Postage and
packing is always completely Free.
There is no obligation or commitment —
you receive books only for
as long as you want to.

**It's easy! Fill in the coupon below and return it to
MILLS & BOON READER SERVICE, FREEPOST, P.O. BOX 236,
CROYDON, SURREY CR9 9EL.**

**Please note: READERS IN SOUTH AFRICA write to
Mills & Boon Ltd., Postbag X3010,
Randburg 2125, S. Africa.**

- -

FREE BOOKS CERTIFICATE

**To: Mills & Boon Reader Service, FREEPOST, P.O. Box 236,
Croydon, Surrey CR9 9EL.**

Please send me, free and without obligation, four Dr. Nurse Romances, and reserve a
Reader Service Subscription for me. If I decide to subscribe I shall receive, following my free
parcel of books, eight new Dr. Nurse Romances every two months for £8.00, post and
packing free. If I decide not to subscribe, I shall write to you within 10 days. The free books
are mine to keep in any case. I understand that I may cancel my subscription at any time
simply by writing to you. I am over 18 years of age.
Please write in BLOCK CAPITALS.

Name _____

Address _____

_____

_____ Postcode _____

SEND NO MONEY — TAKE NO RISKS

EP11D